Quivering desire

Copyright @ 2025

All Rights Reserved

Published by

ISBN: 978-1-0689798-7-3

"Pleasure wasn't the goal
—it was the language,
the battlefield, and the
answer."

Table of Contents

Just a Drink

I wasn't supposed to be out tonight. But something inside me itched—deep, restless, hungry. I needed air. I needed out.

I didn't live alone. Not even close.

I was hemmed in by noise that never ends—the low static of the TV no one was really watching, the anxious hum of the fridge, the ever-present ticking of a life too carefully constructed.

I had built it all, piece by piece: the job, the apartment, the calendar coloured in with precision, a life that looked good from the outside.

But on the inside?

I was quiet in the wrong places.

Something was missing. A beat that never drops. A touch that never came.

The firm I worked for had booked Damien a room at the hotel where the weekend seminar was also taking place.

One of my subordinates, technically. But Damien was new to the firm and never felt like just another line on the payroll.

The hotel was close to my apartment— a thirty-minute walk, or maybe a little more if I strolled.

And I started thinking about the quiet.

The low hum of the city pressing its lips onto the night.

The way hotel lights cast shadows like secrets.

And the way I needed to slip into one of them.

I told myself I might meet a couple of clients. Have a drink. Talk business.

I always say that when I want to feel reckless without admitting I'm chasing something.

And tonight, it wasn't about business.

There was something about the air—charged, alive, like a whisper against skin before the kiss lands.

I needed to feel different.

To lose myself for a moment in something unscheduled.

Unpredictable.

Undone.

So, I did what I wasn't supposed to do. I snuck out— softly, silently, like desire slipping past reason, wearing intention and a hint of naughtiness.

No goodbyes. No explanations. Just the familiar sound of my door closing behind me and the click of my heels falling into step with a city that didn't ask questions.

I didn't even think about Damien.

Not exactly.

It wasn't about him, not yet.

It was about what he represented:

a what-if,

a soft detour off the straight and narrow.

A door cracked open in a hallway I didn't know I wanted to walk down.

And somewhere between the streetlight and the lobby, my pulse started to race.

I walked through the lobby like I owned the night when I arrived.

Not rushed. Not hesitant.

Each step measured, heels kissing the marble floor with a quiet kind of command.

I wasn't just another woman ducking into the bar for a drink— I was Liz, a corporate lawyer, partner.

Poised. Sharp. Untouchable.

Or so I told myself.

I slid onto a barstool and ordered a glass of red, letting the stem settle between my fingers like an extension of my mood. The wine came quickly, rich, deep, and dark as desire.

I took a sip. Let it linger.

Let it stain my lips with something close to confidence.

The room hummed with half-hearted flirtations and practiced laughs.

I offered mine in return: small talk, polished smiles, the easy charm of someone who knew how to play the game.

But I wasn't really there for that.

My mind kept drifting to him.

To Damien.

The very thought sent a flicker of heat coiling low in my belly.

I hadn't planned to seek him out.

But the bar was too small for secrets.

Too intimate for pretending.

And then—there he was.

Leaning against the far end of the bar, one hand resting on the polished wood, the other curled casually around a glass.

Relaxed. Composed. Dangerously self-assured.

He saw me.

Of course, he did.

And when our eyes met, it was like everything else dropped away.

The clinking glasses. The background music. The murmur of voices.

All I could hear was the space between us tightening.

His gaze didn't wander. It didn't question.

I just held mine—steady, slow, and thick, with implications.

He didn't wait for an invitation.

Maybe he didn't need one.

He moved toward me like it had already been decided.

Like he knew.

And when he reached me, that smile—that quiet curve of his lips—said everything neither of us dared to speak.

Not yet.

"Liz," he said, voice like warm velvet, poured low and slow into the space between us.

"Didn't expect to see you here."

My name sounded different from his lips—less like just a name and more like a secret.

And for a second, I forgot how to breathe.

I should've said something safe. Something professional.

But that part of me—the one that wears tailored suits and speaks in bullet points—had already gone quiet.

What answered was something softer, bolder, and a little reckless.

"Just... needed a drink," I said, the shrug of my shoulder masking the pulse in my throat. "Figured I might as well make an appearance before tomorrow."

He nodded slowly. Considered.

"That makes sense."

But the look he gave me said something else entirely.

That smile—it wasn't loud. It didn't need to be. It curled at the corners of his mouth like he was in on a secret, and I was part of it.

We talked.

At first, it was easy—work, the seminar, harmless banter.

But under it all, something kept shifting.

The air grew warmer and more intimate as if the whole bar had tilted just a little to draw us closer.

He laughed at something I said, leaned in, and suddenly, the distance between our bodies didn't feel like enough.

There was something about Damien—something that didn't ask permission.

He didn't speak to "Liz from senior management."

He spoke to me.

Just me.

And I felt it.

The way his gaze lingered just a beat longer than necessary.

The way his voice dipped when he said my name again, as if he knew it was stirring something beneath my skin.

I wasn't just sitting at a hotel bar anymore.

I was seen.

Not as a title.

Not as a polished version of myself built for boardrooms and leadership reviews.

But as a woman.

One with fire in her veins and hunger tightening low in her belly.

And he looked at me like he was ready to taste every flicker of it.

As the evening stretched on, the wine kept finding its way to our glasses—one, then two, then three.

And with every slow sip, something slipped.

Not just the formalities, but the quiet rules I'd lived by. The ones that kept me composed. Controlled. Safe.

We leaned in, inch by inch, as though gravity had shifted.

His voice was softer now, and mine was warmer.

The conversation strayed from its professional focus and began to drift into something more personal.

Tender.

Tempting.

Somewhere between laughter and silence, we crossed an invisible line.

I couldn't tell you when, only that it happened—how we went from colleagues to something more elemental.

Two people circling something unspoken, each word daring the other to come closer.

The air between us felt charged, as if a storm was building beneath our skin.

And I could feel the heat—low and quiet at first, like a flicker behind my ribs.

But it grew.

It lived in the way his eyes didn't just look at me—they held me.

It was evident in the way his smile curved, as if he already knew how this night would end.

I should have left.

Pushed back from the bar, made some excuse, drew that line back where it belonged. I should've left this as a fantasy.

But I didn't.

I stayed.

And in that still, charged moment, it was no longer about the wine or the seminar.

It was about how he made me feel—like a woman standing at the edge of something dangerous.

And delicious.

He said something—I don't remember what.

Some half-joke, some throwaway line meant to keep the moment light.

But his hand brushed against mine as he reached for his glass, and suddenly, nothing felt light at all.

It was barely a touch.

A whisper of skin on skin.

But it felt like thunder beneath the surface of my body.

I didn't move. Didn't flinch.

I just let my fingers rest there, close enough to feel his pulse, and close enough to know this wasn't just in my head.

He noticed.

God, he noticed.

His eyes flicked to our hands, then back to mine, searching for permission he didn't need to ask for.

And I gave it.

With a breath. A look. The smallest nod.

That was all it took.

His fingers slid over mine, warm, firm.

Purposeful.

He held my hand like he'd done it before in some dream neither of us dared speak aloud.

And I let him.

I let that touch bloom through me, a slow ache that travelled all the way to my knees.

For a moment, the bar disappeared.

The clinking glasses, the scattered laughter, the curated charm of public space—none of it existed.

Just this.

Just us.

And when I looked up, when I saw the way his eyes had darkened—like he'd made a decision, like he already knew how the next hour would unfold—

I felt something shift in me.

Something deeper.

Hungrier.

This wasn't curiosity anymore.

It wasn't just flirting.

This was desire.

And it had finally been touched.

Damien was relaxed.

And I could feel it—the shift.

It was as if the weight of expectations had lifted from his shoulders the moment he realized I wasn't playing the boss anymore.

I wasn't the one giving orders, keeping things stiff and formal. No, I was just me, loosened up and relaxed.

And so was he.

It felt good.

We still talked about work, of course. What else could we talk about? But the air between us was different now.

Sharper, playful, like we were sharing some secret joke that only we could understand.

We bantered about the competition, defending our firm with a kind of casual bravado that felt oddly liberating.

It was like I'd let go of the leash I'd kept so tight around myself, and Damien—he wasn't just a colleague anymore. He was someone I could share this with.

Not Liz, a partner at the law firm he worked at, but just Liz. Someone who could talk, laugh, and let go of the rules that had always kept us apart.

We were holding hands.

And I couldn't remember the last time I had felt this vulnerable.

This exposed.

But the thing was, it didn't feel forced.

It didn't feel wrong.

It felt natural.

Right.

Like the touch of his fingers had unlocked something inside me that I didn't even know I'd been hiding.

And now that it was open, I couldn't bear to close it.

Before I knew it, we were laughing again—close, easy, and sharing whispered jokes like we were in on something no one else could understand. The air around us felt charged, electric. And then, in one careless moment, I tipped my glass, the red wine splashing across my chest and down my dress.

I froze. My heart skipped, the humiliation surging through me. The deep crimson liquid soaked into the fabric, staining it in a way I couldn't ignore. My mind screamed for a solution, but all I could do was stand there, looking like a fool.

And then Damien—he didn't skip a beat.

"Let me help you." his voice was calm and reassuring, as though this was a familiar scene. It was as if he'd offered this kind of help a thousand times before. There was no awkwardness in his tone, no hesitation—just quiet confidence.

"You can borrow my room to clean up. It's no big deal. No weirdness," he added, his smile wide, comforting—disarming even.

I should've said no. I should've just called a cab and returned to the life I had built—the life I was supposed to live. The life that made sense, that followed the rules.

But I didn't.

I hesitated for only a heartbeat, but it felt like an eternity. I wanted to leave—I knew I should. But something about the way he stood there and the quiet invitation in his eyes made leaving feel wrong.

I couldn't explain it.

So I didn't.

"Alright," I said, the words slipping out, quieter than intended. "Just... give me a minute."

Then we headed upstairs to his room.

The slow hum of the elevator as it climbed felt endless, and with each passing floor, the tension in my chest built. My thoughts scrambled as I raced to make sense of the moment. I wasn't naive—I knew exactly what this could lead to. But still, a strange, unfamiliar pull made my heart beat harder, my skin suddenly too sensitive, too aware of the dim, golden lights flickering above us. Why did it feel like more than just a drink? Why did my body react like this?

When we finally reached his room, Damien opened the door. I stepped inside, my senses firing at once. The room was sterile and simple, like any other hotel room, but something about it made it stand out. It felt private. Intimate, even. A space where no one else had the right to be.

"Make yourself at home," he said, his voice low, but smooth—almost like a promise. "I'll leave you to freshen up."

I nodded, though it felt like my body was moving before my mind had fully caught up. I walked toward the bathroom, the weight of his gaze still lingering on me. Inside, I stood in front of the mirror for a moment, my breath filling the silence. The rush of the evening—the wine, the laughter, the touch—was still buzzing beneath my skin.

I let the cool water run over my hands, splashing my face, trying to steady my pulse. My thoughts were a blur, spinning around the questions I didn't want to ask myself. What was I doing here? What did I want? I could just fix myself, leave, and pretend nothing had happened.

But something told me that walking away wasn't an option. That feeling, the warmth between us, the connection—it was too strong to ignore.

So, I stood there for a moment longer, letting the water run over my hands, focusing on the clarity of the cold droplets, even as the heat inside me continued to build.

I'd be fine. I'd dry my dress, and I'd leave. This wasn't anything serious.

And my body knew better.

But I wasn't prepared for what I saw when I stepped out.

Damien stood by the bed, his shirt discarded, revealing a sculpted and toned body, his skin gleaming under the soft light of the room. He was about to slide under the covers when I walked into view, and at that moment, everything in the world seemed to be still.

My breath caught, trapped in my chest.

He turned toward me, and his gaze locked with mine. The darkness in his eyes deepened, and I could feel the weight of his stare like a touch, pulling at me. I froze. My heart thudded, not sure whether to step back or move closer.

The alcohol in my veins blurred the lines I usually kept so carefully drawn, but it didn't matter. Not anymore.

The tension between us was palpable, thickening the air with a kind of raw electricity I couldn't deny. I could feel every part of my body screaming for something more, something I hadn't been able to admit, even to myself.

I took a step toward him.

And then, in a blur of sudden clumsiness, my feet betrayed me. I lost my balance, pitching forward into the air.

I braced myself, but his arms were there before I could fall. Strong hands caught me—steady, unyielding—lifting me back to my feet as if I weighed nothing.

I could feel the warmth of his body close to mine, the strength of his touch seeping into my skin. My pulse thundered in my ears, drowning out everything else, leaving only the two of us in the room's silence.

We stood there for a breathless moment, suspended in time. His eyes searched mine, a flicker of hesitation in their depth. A question, an unspoken uncertainty.

I thought I'd only come in, freshen up, and leave. That was the plan. But from the moment I stepped out of the bathroom, everything had changed.

He was now staring at me, but not just looking—his gaze was intense, searching, almost as if he was waiting for something.

Testing me.

Daring me to cross a line I hadn't even known existed.

Then he moved closer—slowly, deliberately, as if every step mattered less than the magnetic pull between us. He reached out, his fingers grazing the edge of my dress. The touch was light but unmistakable, sending a jolt of electricity straight through me. It was the kind of touch that made my skin tingle, that made every nerve stand at attention.

I wasn't sure what I was doing—if I was following some deep-seated instinct or simply surrendering to the pull that had been building between us all evening. But whatever it was, I didn't pull away. Instead, I leaned in, just a little closer, my breath a bit shakier than usual, my body suddenly hyper-aware of the space between us.

Damien's hands slid over the fabric of my dress, pushing it up, inch by inch. I let him, feeling each movement of his hands like they were caressing my very soul. As the fabric pooled around my waist, I shivered, feeling exposed but not afraid. His eyes met mine again, dark with something I couldn't name, and I could feel my heart pounding.

His fingers brushed across the lace of my underwear, and it felt like every nerve in my body was on fire. I wasn't sure if it was the wine, the heat of the room, or something more primal, but every touch, every moment felt like it was stretching time, pulling us deeper into this unspoken thing we were both feeling.

When my panties slid off, the world felt even quieter, like there was only us in the world. The cool air against my bare skin contrasted sharply with the heat rising between us. I didn't know what I was doing, but I didn't want it to stop.

And then, without another word, I found myself wrapped around him. My legs instinctively circled his waist, and I could feel the strength in his arms as he lifted me with ease, as though I were weightless in his embrace. The room spun for a second, but I didn't care.

The next thing I knew, we were moving, his body aligned with mine in the most intimate way possible. Every kiss and every touch felt like my first time—electric, thrilling, intense. There was no rush, no frantic urgency, just the slow, deliberate rhythm of two bodies finding perfect harmony.

I felt my pulse quicken, my body moving with his, responding to the way he held me, the way he kissed me. The world outside no longer existed. Nothing mattered but him, but the feel of his hands on my skin, the warmth of his breath, the way he made me feel like I could be anyone, anywhere—so utterly alive.

For a moment, time didn't matter. There were no lines, no professional boundaries, no expectations. There was just us, tangled in the quiet chaos of this stolen moment. And as we moved together, I realized that maybe I wasn't running away from anything. Perhaps I was finally letting myself feel, really feel, for the first time in a long time.

I barely had time to catch my breath before Damien's hands found my hips, fingers digging in with delicious intent. His touch was firm, guiding, unapologetically in control, yet a tenderness beneath it made my body tremble.

He led me to the fireplace, the heat of the flames licking at our skin as though they, too, were hungry for what was about to happen. My body felt suspended between worlds—weightless, yet grounded by the gravity of his presence.

Before I could process the next heartbeat, he bent me forward, palms flat against the warm stone, the flicker of firelight dancing across my skin. I gasped as his body pressed against mine—thick, hot, and demanding. His hands positioned me just so, a quiet command pulsing through every movement. And then—

He entered me.

It was one long, steady thrust that knocked the air from my lungs and replaced it with a moan I didn't recognize as my own. He filled me completely, the stretch intoxicating, dizzying. My body pulsed around him, greedy and alive, and he began to move.

Slow at first.

Deep.

Delicious.

Then harder. Faster. Relentless.

Each thrust sent sparks up my spine, his hips slamming against me in rhythm with my cries—low, broken things that filled the room like music only he could hear. He grunted behind me, the sound raw and deep, and it only pushed me closer to the edge.

I braced myself, fingers curled into the stone, back arched, as he took me without hesitation. Every snap of his hips made me unravel a little more, made me needier, louder, closer.

"Damien—" I choked out his name, a prayer and a plea.

"You're mine," he growled into the curve of my neck, and I shattered on those words alone.

My orgasm hit like fire—sudden, consuming, a burst of pleasure so intense I nearly collapsed. He followed with a strangled curse, thrusting one final time as he spilled into me, hips twitching as he came, still pulsing deep inside.

We stayed that way momentarily, panting, clinging to the edge of bliss. And then he gathered me into his arms, lifting me gently and carrying me to the bed.

The sheets were cool against our flushed skin as we collapsed, tangled together in a breathless heap. My head rested on his chest, my fingers lazily tracing the sweat-slick lines of his abdomen. The room was quiet, but our bodies still hummed from the aftershock.

We didn't speak. We didn't need to.

There was only the soft crackle of the fire and the rise and fall of our breaths—perfectly in sync, like the last notes of a song we hadn't realized we were writing together.

But Damien wasn't done.

Even in the afterglow, with our bodies still slick and tangled in lazy breaths, I felt the shift in his energy—a slow-burning hunger reigniting beneath his skin. His hands moved over me like they knew every inch by heart, but were desperate to rediscover it all again.

A few minutes passed, and he was ready again.

The way he rose behind me, hard and hot once more, made something deep inside me clench with anticipation. I hadn't expected it, but I welcomed it. My body answered him instinctively, drawn to his fire, craving more of the flame we'd barely just extinguished.

He kissed me once, slowly, deeply, possessively—before standing and taking my hand. I followed, legs still shaky, lips swollen from his earlier devotion. He led me to the kitchen counter like a man on a mission, as if each part of the hotel room needed to witness what we were becoming.

Without a word, he lifted me effortlessly.

It was as though the only thing that mattered was getting me exactly where he wanted me. I gasped as my back hit the cool edge of the counter, a shock against the fever of my skin. One leg was hoisted up, bent at the knee and anchored around his waist. The other found balance against the floor, toes barely brushing the tile.

And then, he entered me again.

The new angle made it sharper and deeper. "More!" I cried out, one hand gripping the edge of the counter while the other clutched his shoulder. His eyes never left mine, and I saw everything—want, reverence, power in that gaze.

"Look at me," he said, voice low, thick with heat.

I did.

God, I did.

Because the way he filled me, moved inside me, demanded it. His thrusts were deliberate and paced like he was trying to draw every sound, every tremor, every reaction out of me one by one. I was open for him—laid bare and trembling. Every time he pushed forward, I felt like I was unravelling all over again.

The slap of skin against skin echoed in the quiet hotel room, broken only by my soft moans and his breath in my ear. He wasn't just taking me—he was claiming me in every space we occupied.

And I wanted it.

My fingers raked through his hair as I pulled him closer, our foreheads pressed together now. Sweat beaded down his temple. My lips brushed his. The moment held between us like suspended heat—so intimate, so intense it almost ached.

He groaned against my mouth, deeper now, faster—building toward something inevitable. I clenched around him, my own release swelling inside me like a wave ready to crash.

"Don't stop," I whispered, breathless, on the edge of breaking again.

And he didn't.

He took me right there, with a fierce passion that nearly shattered me, holding me steady with hands that knew both force and care. And when I finally tipped over the edge, it felt like falling through fire and floating through silk all at once.

My name left his lips like a vow.

His name echoed in mine like worship.

And then we stilled—foreheads pressed, hearts racing, bodies still fused and trembling.

In that small hotel room with nothing but the hum of the fridge and the rhythm of our breath between us, I felt it —that beautiful, dangerous high of needing someone so completely.

The dopamine rush.

We stayed there for a while, still joined, barely breathing, like the world had shrunk to this moment—sweaty skin, parted lips, racing hearts. I thought maybe that was it. That we'd finally reached the peak, that this was the fall after the high.

But Damien's fingers drifted.

Soft at first, grazing the inside of my thigh, then trailing higher, coaxing another gasp from my chest. My body, already hypersensitive, pulsed with renewed awareness. My breath hitched when he shifted, still inside me, moving just slightly—but enough to stir the embers.

I glanced at him, wide-eyed, the look in his darkened gaze making it clear: he wasn't done.

Neither was I.

With a wicked smirk, he swept me off the counter and into his arms like I was something precious that couldn't be left behind. He carried me to the space between the bed and the fireplace, setting me down gently onto the plush rug in front of the fireplace.

And then, he knelt between my legs.

That same heat, aching hunger, surged back into the room, into my chest, into the places he'd just left worshipped and sore. He hovered over me, teasing, kissing his way along my inner thigh until I squirmed, until I whispered his name like a plea.

But he took his time.

He watched my face as his lips descended, as his tongue flicked softly, then deliberately, over where I was already throbbing for him. My back arched off the rug, breath catching in my throat, as waves of pleasure rolled back in with devastating grace. He knew me now—my every sound, every movement, every tightening muscle—and he wielded that knowledge with devastating precision.

He devoured me like he had all the time in the world.

Like my pleasure was the only thing that mattered.

And just as I was about to break, he got back up, sliding into me once more with a smooth, aching push that made my eyes flutter shut and a sharp cry escape my throat. His body moulded to mine—hips pressed to hips, chest against chest, his forehead resting on mine.

The rhythm was different now.

Not frenzied. Not hard.

This was slow.

Deep.

Consuming.

He held my face in both hands and kissed me while we moved together in perfect sync, each roll of his hips drawing soft whimpers from me. It was like we were melting into one another—like the lines between where I ended and he began no longer mattered.

And then he whispered it.

Right against my lips.

"My god, the way you feel... I don't want to let go."

That did it.

That sent me over again—this time softer, deeper, with tears in my eyes and a shiver in my limbs as I fell apart beneath him. He followed, burying himself in me with one final groan, raw and undone, before collapsing beside me.

We became tangled together, breathless, slick, and utterly spent.

And this time—it really was the end.

A slow, blissful descent after a storm that had shaken us both to the core.

Wrapped in each other's arms on the rug, the glow of the fire dancing over our skin, we didn't need to speak. Everything had already been said in the way our bodies had reached, given, and surrendered.

He kissed my shoulder, softly now.

I closed my eyes, letting the warmth of his embrace and the quiet pulse between my legs lull me into something close to sleep.

We were more than just a hook-up at that moment.

We were fire and rhythm.

And silence.

And stillness.

And whatever came after this—well, that was for Monday.

We stayed there, skin pressed to skin, our bodies humming with the echo of everything we'd just shared. The fire had dwindled to a soft glow, casting amber shadows across the room. I nestled closer to him, letting the rise and fall of his chest soothe the flutter still in mine.

He didn't speak. Neither did I.

Words would've ruined it.

Instead, we let the silence stretch, warm and thick, like a blanket draped over our tangled limbs. I traced lazy circles along his chest, memorizing the feel of him—the way his skin curved, the way his pulse beat beneath my fingertips. Every part of me still ached, but it was a beautiful ache, one that reminded me just how thoroughly he had claimed me.

I had snuck out of my home and left the safety of my little world behind, but in that moment, none of it mattered. All that mattered was this—this raw, unapologetic connection with him. And as I closed my eyes, wrapped in his arms, I realized that I had never felt so alive, so at peace, as I did right then.

I should have felt guilty.

Maybe I did, in some quiet corner of my mind. But it was drowned out by the fire still flickering in my veins. By the way he tightened his arm around me as if he could read my thoughts and didn't want me to slip away just yet.

And I didn't want to.

I wanted to stay in this cocoon of post-passion haze. Let the scent of us cling to my skin. Let the memory of his touch mark me from the inside out. My body was his for now, but something deeper had shifted, too.

I felt… changed.

Not broken. Not reckless.

Empowered.

Like I'd taken something for myself, something that belonged to me and me alone. No permission. No explanations. Just a moment of pure, undeniable want— and the courage to chase it.

Morning Glory

The soft light of Saturday morning crept through the curtains, its golden rays brushing across the room and warming my skin. My eyes fluttered open slowly, and for a moment, everything felt peaceful. Almost too peaceful.

But then I felt it—a stir beneath me, a reminder of last night. Damien. My body was still pressed against his, his warmth surrounding me. I hadn't meant to fall asleep like this, not like this, tangled in the aftermath of what we had shared. But here I was, his arms wrapped tightly around me, his body still holding onto me like it didn't want to let go.

The more I held onto Damien, the more I wanted him.

It wasn't just the warmth of our bodies under the sheets or the soft pull of dawn light sneaking through the curtains—it was something more profound. Something that pulsed beneath my skin, stirred low in my belly, and burned just beneath my breath.

Damien was already awake—or if he wasn't, his body certainly was. He was throbbing with anticipation, the thick heat of him pressed against me, unmistakable and impossible to ignore. I shifted slightly, just enough for the softest friction, and heard the way his breath hitched behind me. That sound alone sent a ripple of heat down my spine.

We didn't say a word.

We didn't have to.

Our bodies had already spoken the night before—cried out, demanded, whispered—and now, we picked up right where we left off with the hush of early morning cloaking us.

His hand slid slowly over my hip, tracing the curve like he was rediscovering a place he'd only begun to map. The sheets rustled as he shifted behind me, fitting us together in a way that felt effortless, inevitable. I was already open to him—ready—and when he slid into me from behind, it was like a breath I'd been holding finally released.

Slow. Deep. Intimate.

The kind of rhythm that didn't rush but smouldered.

He filled me with an aching slowness that sent sparks through my nerves, and I pressed back against him, greedy for more but unwilling to break the spell of our silent communion. It wasn't frenzied, not yet. It was reverent, like we were worshiping something sacred in one another.

My fingers gripped the pillow as he moved, slow at first, drawing out every sensation. Each thrust was deliberate, controlled, and devastating. I bit my lip to keep quiet, but my body betrayed me—rocking back, clenching around him, needing more and craving it.

He must've felt it too, the way my hunger flared, because he reached around and cupped my breast, his thumb brushing my nipple in a way that made me moan. His lips found my shoulder, trailing kisses that only added to the fire curling low and tight inside me.

Then his voice, low and rough: "You feel like a dream in the morning."

And I did. I felt like something wild and untamed, like this moment didn't belong to the real world at all. Just us. Just this. Lost in the heat and hush of a new day.

He quickened, slowly, teasing us both to the edge of losing control, and I let myself fall into the rhythm, into the burn, into him.

Damien didn't rush.

He knew exactly what he was doing—how to pull my body closer, how to keep me hovering just on the edge of unravelling. His pace was maddening in the best way— steady, purposeful, with every deep thrust pulling a sigh, a whisper, a silent plea from my lips.

The morning was quiet, but inside me, a storm was building.

Each brush of his skin against mine sparked something electric. His hand trailed down my thigh, fingers grazing the sensitive crease where my leg met my hip, then curling to grip me firmly. He pulled me back against him, deeper, fuller—and I gasped. My breath hitched, the sound raw in the quiet room, and his body responded with a soft, low growl against my neck.

Still, he didn't speed up.

Instead, he bent forward, his chest to my back, and the heat of his mouth met my ear.

"You're trying to stay quiet." His voice was thick with control, amusement, and desire. "But I want to hear you."

That undid something in me.

His hand slid upward again, tracing every inch of my skin like he wanted to memorize the shape of my need. His fingers found the place where I was already aching for more attention, and when he touched me there, slow, firm, knowing—I almost came undone. I pressed my face into the pillow, whimpering, trying to ride it out, but he was relentless in his patience.

"Damien…" I breathed. It was the only word I could manage, and even that felt like a surrender.

He turned me around and got on top of me, hummed, pleased, his rhythm still slow but impossibly deep, every motion timed like he was composing music in the way he made me feel. My body clenched around him, eager, over-eager, and his hand tightened at my hip like he could feel it too—how close I was getting, how much I wanted to let go.

But I didn't.

Not yet.

I held on—barely—teetering on the edge he kept me dancing along.

And God, it was beautiful.

His breath was hot on my neck, and his hands—God, his hands—moved like he owned every part of me. Not with rush, not with brute force, but with absolute certainty. Damien was sculpting me with his touch, learning me, teasing every nerve to the surface until I was trembling.

He shifted just slightly, and the new angle made me gasp —sharp, involuntary.

He stilled.

"Right there?" he whispered, his voice velvet-wrapped dominance.

I nodded, unable to speak, and he rewarded me with a slow, deliberate roll of his hips, right there, exactly where I needed him. It was almost cruel, how good it felt. Like every time he withdrew, I lost a little more of myself— until the only thing grounding me was the friction of his body and the sound of our mingled breathing.

I gripped the sheets, clawed at the pillow, anything to anchor myself. But it was no use.

I was weightless.

His hand slid beneath me, parting my thighs a little more, lifting my hips just enough to deepen everything. The change made me cry out—quietly, needily, desperately. I bit my lip to muffle the sound, and he caught it.

"No," he murmured, lips against my ear. "Don't hide that from me. I want to hear what I'm doing to you."

His words hit me like a shockwave, ricocheting down my spine and straight into the molten ache between my legs. I arched into him, needing more, more, and he responded with another deep, steady thrust, grinding just right.

My thighs trembled.

My breath stuttered.

But he still didn't let me fall.

He kept me there—on that razor edge of pleasure and restraint—each movement pushing me closer, then pulling me back. My body was a livewire, stretched taut, trembling with the weight of anticipation.

"Damien…" I breathed again, this time less a plea, more a confession.

He kissed my shoulder, my neck—claiming every inch of me with heat and adoration. "Not yet," he said softly. "You're going to remember this every time you close your eyes."

And I already knew he was right.

Every inch of me was brimming with sensation, pulsing with need so sharp it bordered on unbearable. Damien moved with that same devastating patience—each stroke deliberate, each pause just long enough to make me gasp, to make me feel. He was stringing me along a delicate thread, and I was powerless in his hands, unravelling one gasp, one moan at a time.

I clung to him—not just with fingers, but with everything in me. My hips lifted to meet his every movement, chasing the rhythm he refused to let fully break loose. It was maddening, how much control he had—not over me, but over the space between us. Over the build.

And oh, the build was sweet torture.

My nails sank into his shoulders, my legs wrapped tighter around him, my whole body humming, shaking, needing—and still he didn't let me fall.

He kissed me again, slower this time, with a tenderness that somehow made the burn inside me even worse. His lips tasted like possession, like worship, like a silent promise that whatever this was, it was more than lust.

Our bodies moved in sync, not fast, not wild—just deep. Controlled. Poised on the edge of the inferno. Every thrust was a tease. Every breath was a dare.

I opened my eyes and found his already watching me— those stormy eyes, dark with desire and something else. Something I didn't dare name just yet. Something that made my chest feel tight and my pulse race in a whole different way.

"Say it," he whispered, brushing his lips against mine, barely touching but making me feel everything. "Tell me what you want."

My voice was barely a breath, but it came out, raw and shaking: "You."

His name caught in my throat, a whisper turned moan, as the last of my resistance melted into the sheets. His hands held me like I was something precious and wild all at once—fingers splayed across my hips, anchoring me, owning me. There was no hiding now. No more teasing. Just that slow, exquisite surrender that bloomed from my spine to the tips of my fingers.

He moved deeper, slower, as though he wanted to memorize every sensation. Every part of me was bare to him—body, breath, soul—and somehow that vulnerability didn't make me feel small. It made me feel seen.

Our mouths found each other again, and the kiss was all heat and adoration. There was no rush, no desperation, just a quiet intensity that said, "We're here, and we're not letting go."

My legs trembled against his sides, and his hand slid up to my ribs, fingers brushing under my breast like a question. I arched into him with a quiet answer, letting him know that yes, I was his. Here. Now. Entirely.

His forehead dropped against mine. "You feel…" he started, but then his voice caught, and he groaned deep in his chest instead.

That sound made something deep in me clench, and I held him tighter, like we could merge completely if I just stayed close enough. Every breath he took against my cheek lit another fire under my skin.

We were still moving, but it wasn't frantic. It was like dancing at the edge of something sacred, stretching that line between control and chaos, both of us refusing to rush what was too beautiful to break.

And I didn't want it to end. Not yet.

Not when surrender had never felt so safe.

His rhythm deepened, the slow drag of his body over mine grounding us both, like the world had narrowed to nothing but touch and sound—our breath, our heartbeat, the soft creak of the bed as we moved in tandem.

Damien's grip tightened just slightly, anchoring me as he shifted, angling himself with intention. My gasp filled the space between us—it was different, deeper, and it hit something in me that made my back arch and my fingers dig into his shoulders. He moaned into my neck, a low, reverent sound, and I could feel the tension rising in both of us like a tide that couldn't be held back any longer.

He whispered my name against my skin—soft, worshipful—and I shattered.

My body trembled beneath him, a wave of release crashing through me so powerfully it stole my breath. And still, he moved, carrying me through it, pulling every last tremor from my limbs until I was nothing but sensation and surrender.

Then his breath hitched, his body stilled, and he followed, gripping me like I was the only thing tethering him to the earth as he let go completely. His release was raw, full-bodied, a groan that melted into my mouth as he kissed me through the end of it.

We didn't move for a long time. Just lay there—limbs tangled, chests heaving, skin slick with the proof of everything we'd given each other. The world outside our little cocoon could've been on fire, and neither of us would've noticed.

Wrapped in the quiet glow of the aftermath, he tucked a strand of hair behind my ear and kissed my forehead, murmuring something soft I didn't catch but felt down to my bones.

I had never felt more undone. Or more whole.

As the moment of intimacy passed and the silence settled between us, a strange clarity washed over me. The room felt quieter now, the air heavy but not uncomfortable. We were both lying there, side by side, wrapped in the warmth of each other's presence, yet both of us fully aware of the boundaries that had just been crossed, again.

Damien shifted, propping himself up on one elbow to look at me. I met his gaze, a mix of emotions swirling in my chest—embarrassment, excitement, guilt—but above all, a sense of exhilaration that seemed to be coursing through me, making it hard to focus on anything else.

There was a moment of silence, during which we both digested what had happened and its implications. I could feel the lingering heat between us, but the initial rush was starting to calm down. We were both sober now, and the weight of the last 12 hours seemed to settle in, leaving a bit of an uncomfortable feeling, like the morning after an indulgence you knew you'd enjoy, but wondered how you'd explain it to anyone else.

Still, that embarrassment didn't seem to matter much in the grand scheme of things. I was high on dopamine, floating in the afterglow of a morning glory, and for now, it was enough to simply share this unspoken understanding with him. The world outside the room seemed distant and irrelevant.

As the tension in the room slowly dissipated, I couldn't help but smile at the absurdity of it all. I had snuck out, had this unexpected and unforgettable night, and now, all I could do was lie there, laughing inwardly at how quickly things had changed. But despite all the uncertainty, there was a sense of peace about it. For now, I was content to let it be our secret.

After all, sometimes life needs a little spontaneity, a little reckless indulgence. And the previous 12 hours had undoubtedly been one of those moments.

Afternoon Delight

I went home early in the morning and got ready for the day. It wasn't pretty because I couldn't explain where I had spent the night, but that didn't bother me once I got back to the hotel for the seminar.

Now, I hadn't even given my presentation yet, but I was already a wreck.

I stood in the greenroom, pretending to review my notes one last time, but the truth? My body was humming with memories that had nothing to do with keynote slides or quarterly projections. Damien had rooted himself deep in my head—and lower—and nothing I did could shake the pull.

I adjusted my blouse again, tugging the fabric like it could somehow erase the ghost of his touch. But it clung to me, that memory—his lips trailing down my neck, his fingers skating the edges of places I was still throbbing from. Every inhale made me remember. Every exhale made me want.

I wasn't nervous about the presentation. I was supposed to be polished, commanding, and ready to lead. But my pulse said otherwise. It beat against my skin like it had heard secrets my mouth hadn't dared speak aloud. I checked my reflection, fixed a flyaway strand of hair and touched up my lip colour, pretending to be thorough.

But inside, I was burning.

Because all morning, I hadn't been able to stop replaying last night, the way Damien had touched me like he couldn't help himself. The way I had responded was like I'd been waiting for him all my life.

The hotel room. The fireplace. His voice in my ear, low and ruined with lust. My legs were around him. The urgency. The release. The peace. The fire.

I bit my lip, not from nerves, but to ground myself. To stop the twitch of a smile that was definitely not professional. Because I kept thinking about how Damien had looked at me when I finally collapsed against him, like I was more than a moment.

God, I needed to focus.

I took a breath. It didn't help.

I tried to run my lines silently, but halfway through the intro, his hands were already under my blouse in my imagination again. I squeezed my thighs together, but it was no use. I could still feel him.

A knock on the door pulled me back to reality. It was just a staffer letting me know I had five minutes.

Five minutes to look like I hadn't spent all morning high on dopamine, soaked in memory and wanting more.

Five minutes to pull myself together and pretend that last night didn't unravel me in all the best and worst ways.

And somewhere in the room beyond that door… Damien was waiting.

And I was afraid one look would undo me all over again.

When the time finally came, I stood up and walked to the front like I had done a hundred times before—heels sharp, spine straight, smile polished into place. On the outside, I looked every bit the partner at a law firm, ready to deliver. But inside? I was a storm barely contained by lipstick and willpower.

I launched into my presentation, the words leaving my lips out of muscle memory more than presence of mind. I hit the opening slide and began weaving through the numbers, the jargon I usually used like a blade. But everything felt… flat. My voice was steady, but my brain was foggy. I could hear myself speaking, but it didn't sound like me.

Then it happened.

My eyes found Damien in the crowd.

And just like that, I was off script.

He wasn't doing anything, really. Just sitting there, calm, composed, his focus razor-sharp—on me. But the second our eyes locked, a low, deep, and dangerous current jolted through me. I stumbled over a line, pretended to glance at my notes. My heart was thudding in my ears, and suddenly the conference room felt ten degrees warmer.

God, he looked good. Confident, a little smug, like he knew exactly what he'd done to me. And the worst part? I wanted him to know. I wanted to rewind time and throw myself at him all over again.

But this? This was my space. My name was on the agenda. And I was supposed to own it.

So I kept talking.

I talked through my dry mouth and the sweat building at the base of my spine. I forced my eyes to the slides, to the back wall, to anywhere but Damien.

But my body betrayed me every time I glanced back— every time his gaze touched mine. My breath would hitch. My skin would flush. I'd forget what slide I was on, lose the thread of my argument, fumble a phrase I'd rehearsed.

It was humiliating. And exhilarating.

I hated that he made me feel this way—like some infatuated intern who couldn't keep her hormones in check. I hated that I loved it even more.

Somewhere deep down, a part of me whispered that I was losing control. And it wasn't wrong.

But as I stood there, clutching a remote I could barely focus on, I also realized something else:

Maybe… just maybe, I didn't want it back.

After fumbling through the final few slides and fielding a couple of soft questions, I did what any self-respecting woman on the edge would do—I smiled, nodded, and excused myself with as much grace as I could scrape together. My legs were shaking, but I didn't want to show it.

I wasn't sure where I was going. I just needed to move. Needed to breathe.

And like a shadow trailing me through the haze, Damien followed. Of course he did. He knew I was teetering.

I thought I'd go outside, get some air, maybe even call it a day and disappear into the city. But my feet didn't follow the script. Instead, they led me to the elevator, almost like they had a mind of their own. I stood there, blinking at the chrome doors like they held the answer to whatever the hell I was feeling.

The funny thing is, if I really wanted to freshen up, I could've just ducked into the nearest washroom. I was still dressed for war in my blazer and heels. There was no reason—no reason—for me to be waiting there. None I could admit, anyway.

Until Damien's voice slid in beside me.

"You alright?" he asked, his eyes low and quiet.

I nodded, too fast. Too fake.

He waited a beat, then leaned in just a touch. "Do you want to lie down for a bit?"

My brain screamed, "Hell no!" It pulled up flags, warnings, and every HR clause I'd screamed at my subordinates over office shenanigans. But my body? My body betrayed me. Every nerve screamed, "Hell yes!" The need was overwhelming—raw, electric, and so human it was almost painful.

I didn't say anything right away. I couldn't. I just stared at the little button for the elevator, as if I could press it and be transported somewhere I wasn't responsible, in control, buttoned-up, buttoned-down.

He didn't push. Just stood beside me. Quiet. Close.

The elevator dinged. The doors opened. Still, I didn't move.

And then... I stepped in.

He followed.

The elevator ride was silent.

Not awkward. Not stiff. Just quiet in a way that crackled —like static before a storm. We didn't look at each other, but the air between us was charged, humming. My heart was beating out of rhythm, like it couldn't decide whether to race or pause.

When we stepped into his room, it hit me all over again —how familiar the space already felt, how my body remembered it better than my mind wanted to admit.

I walked in slowly. I wasn't sure if I was supposed to sit, or undress, or say something clever that would make this feel less dangerous. But there was no point pretending I didn't want to be there. My pulse betrayed me. The heat rising beneath my skin betrayed me. The way I stood there, waiting for Damien to make the first move, begged for it.

He closed the door behind us and then leaned against it for a second, just watching me. His eyes weren't hungry—they were searching. It was as if he were checking in, making sure I was still in this with him. That I wouldn't shatter under the weight of my decision.

I took a breath, stepped out of my heels one at a time, and walked toward the edge of the bed. The floor felt soft beneath my feet. The silence between us? Even softer.

"I couldn't focus all morning," I whispered, more to myself than to him. "All I could think about was you."

That's when he crossed the room.

He didn't rush. Didn't speak.

His hands found the edge of my blazer, sliding it off my shoulders like he was unwrapping something precious. And maybe, in that moment, that's exactly how I wanted to feel—like something rare. Wanted. Worth taking time with.

The blazer hit the floor. I didn't care.

He kissed me—slow, deep, and sure. His hands grazed my waist, then held my hips like they were familiar territory. I melted into the moment, into him, into that unspoken yes we both gave each other in the elevator.

And just like that, we weren't colleagues anymore. We weren't in the middle of a seminar weekend. We were just two people tangled up in a quiet storm that had been building since we met.

His mouth moved over mine like he was learning the shape of every sigh I'd been holding back all morning. Every inch he touched sparked something wild under my skin. My lips parted—part shock, part surrender—and his tongue slipped past, soft and warm, pulling a groan straight from my core.

My hands had a mind of their own, unbuttoning his shirt with trembling fingers, one button at a time. The anticipation between each one felt electric—like we were holding back a storm and neither of us wanted to be the first to let it break.

I breathed him in—clean soap, spice, and something distinctly Damien. The scent alone made my knees weak. He eased me backward until the backs of my thighs met the bed. I didn't sit. I stood tall, pressed against him, still half-dressed but completely undone.

"Are you sure?" he asked, his voice barely above a whisper.

"No," I breathed, brushing my lips over his jaw. "But I want it anyway."

That's all it took.

He lifted me effortlessly and laid me down across the bed. His hands ran up the inside of my thighs, the drag of my pencil skirt bunching around my hips. When his fingers found my panties, I was already soaked, already pulsing with need. I gasped as he pressed the fabric aside and traced slow, lazy circles that made me arch off the bed.

"I've been thinking about this since you walked into that seminar," he murmured, kissing down my neck, every word laced with heat. "You looked so buttoned up… but your eyes told a different story."

I moaned, helpless under his touch, every nerve lit up like a city skyline at night. "Shut up and do something about it," I managed to say, my voice thick and needy.

He did.

He slipped his fingers inside, curling just right as his mouth moved to my chest. I pulled him closer, nails dragging down his back, urging him to stop teasing and take me completely.

It was slow, deep, and maddeningly good when he finally did.

I wrapped my legs around him, tilting my hips to meet every slow thrust. Our breaths synced in rhythm, moans mixing with the rustle of sheets and the low hum of the city beyond the window.

The intensity was overwhelming. Beautiful. Dangerous.

And for a moment, I wasn't Liz, the woman with a career, with a reputation to protect. I was just a woman undone—aching, wanting, alive.

He looked at me—really looked at me—and it was as if he suddenly realized how much I was craving him. Not just the pleasure, but him. The way his hands felt on my skin, his flaring hunger, the way his eyes lingered when he thought I wasn't paying attention, and the way my body responded to him like it had been waiting for this exact rhythm.

Damien slowed down. Focused. Every inch of me became his canvas, and he painted with his hands, his mouth, his breath. He moved with purpose, tracing the lines of my body as if he were learning them by heart. Tender, where I was aching for softness. Rough where my hunger was louder than my words. I didn't need to ask—he already knew.

I wasn't just lying beneath him. I was being played. Like a violin—his fingers pulling notes from me I didn't know I could sing. My spine arched to his touch. My breath caught every time he changed tempo. And when he whispered things into my neck—those low, husky words that barely made it past his lips—I felt the music climb, coil, climax.

I wasn't in control anymore. And strangely, I didn't want to be.

For the first time in what felt like forever, I surrendered. Let go of every thought, every mask, every layer of the woman I usually wore so well.

He stripped me down to something raw. And the melody he played was mine.

When the final notes of that beautiful, unscripted melody faded into silence, I lay there beneath him, still, breathless, caught somewhere between reality and a dream I didn't want to wake from. My skin tingled like it had been rewired, like every nerve had been stretched and strummed and now hummed in quiet echo.

Damien didn't say anything at first. He just collapsed beside me, his chest rising and falling, our bodies close but not tangled anymore. The sheets were a mess. The room smelled of skin, sweat, and something sweeter like surrender.

I turned my head to look at him. His eyes were closed, but his lips curled slightly, like he knew exactly what he'd done to me.

And he did.

He reached for my hand without opening his eyes, and I let him take it. Our fingers laced slowly, deliberately. I could feel the rhythm of his pulse against mine, steady now, grounding. He pulled my hand to his chest, like he needed to feel me still there, still real.

Emotion crept in then, like a tide I hadn't seen coming. I felt raw. Not in a bad way, but in that rare, achingly human way that comes when someone's seen too much of you and doesn't look away. I wanted to say something —thank you, or maybe what the hell are we doing?—but the words dissolved before I could form them.

Instead, I tucked into him, let my head rest in the space between his neck and shoulder. His arm curled around me. He kissed my temple—just once—and I swear I felt it bloom all the way to my toes.

Neither of us said it, but we both knew something had shifted.

This wasn't supposed to happen again. It was supposed to be one night, one secret, one beautiful mistake. But now… now, my body remembered every note he played. And worse, my heart had started listening too.

After we were done—again—Damien looked over at me, still catching his breath, and said gently, "You should probably head back."

I groaned and buried my face into the pillow, half-laughing, half-mourning the moment. My limbs felt heavy, like my body had melted into the sheets. I didn't want to move. Not because I was lazy, not even because I was tired. I just… didn't want to leave him. That space. That feeling.

But he was right. I had responsibilities. A seminar still underway, people expecting me, and a very delicate balance to maintain. I peeled myself off the bed with the kind of reluctance that bordered on emotional rebellion. Every part of me wanted to stay in that cocoon. But I got up.

As I freshened up and tried to pull myself back together, I realized something that made my heart skip in the worst way: what I thought would bring closure, some sweet, secret indulgence to tuck away and forget… had actually awakened something. No, unleashed it. A hunger. A boldness. A version of myself I didn't quite recognize—unguarded, reckless, and maybe just a little dangerous.

It was thrilling. It was terrifying.

I stared at my reflection for a beat too long, brushing out my hair and trying to find the version of me that walked in this morning—composed, in control, calculated. But she was gone, and in her place stood a woman who felt like she was flying too close to the sun.

And I wasn't sure I cared if I got burned.

An Electrifying Evening

I couldn't remember the details of the day—what I wore, who I spoke to, how many meetings I sat through. Everything blurred into static behind the one face that refused to leave my thoughts. Damien. His name played on a loop in my mind like a guilty pleasure I didn't want to give up.

I was acting like a thirteen-year-old girl nursing her first big crush, except this wasn't sweet or innocent. It was deeper. Raw. My thoughts weren't butterflies and doodled initials—they were fire. Feverish. I resented the way he had slipped past my defences, taking up space not just in my body but in the places I usually kept guarded. My emotions had never been so easily swayed, and yet… I was enjoying every moment of it.

It wasn't just memory that haunted me. It was sensation. The warmth of his hands, the quiet groans in the back of his throat, the way his breath would hitch when I touched him in just the right place. Sometimes, I'd catch myself staring into space, replaying those moments like my mind was trying to brand them into my body.

I knew I had crossed the line—more than once. Not just with what we'd done, but how often I had mentally gone back to it. Back to him. I'd close my eyes in stolen moments and relive the way his voice dropped when he said my name, the way he looked at me like I was the only thing in the world that mattered. It wasn't just desire anymore. It was obsession, creeping in slowly and silently, curling around my ankles and tugging me deeper every time I swore I'd found my footing.

And worst of all… I didn't want it to stop.

My heart beat faster whenever I thought of being alone with him again. There was this tension coiled inside me, tightly wound and humming with electricity. Every moment apart felt like I was holding my breath, waiting for the next spark, the next chance encounter, the next excuse to close the distance again.

I was in trouble. Delicious, dangerous trouble.

And I was already hoping night would fall quickly.

The seminar ended with the usual mix of handshakes, smiles, and polite nods. I went through the motions, saying the right things and thanking the right people, but it all felt distant, as if I were watching myself from a foggy window. My mind wasn't in the room — it hadn't been all day.

And then I saw him.

Damien.

There he was, standing casually near the back of the room, chatting with someone, hands in his pockets like he had all the time in the world. He wasn't looking at me. He didn't have to. The second I saw him, an electrifying current ran through my body, hot and uninvited, and I had to remind myself — control yourself, Liz.

I kept my pace steady as I walked past him, pretending to be focused on the door. But my body… it had other plans. My hips swayed with too much rhythm, my breath caught in my throat, and even though I didn't look back, I felt him notice. I didn't have to see his smile — I could feel it curl behind me like a heat wave.

I walked as if I might veer off, like I might go left instead of right, back into the crowd instead of towards the exit. But my feet kept moving — away from him, or maybe, in some strange twist, towards him all along.

The lobby was a sea of people, voices rising in a chorus of post-event chatter. I felt a tap on my elbow and turned slightly. It was Damien. His voice low, casual. "Too crowded," he said. "Do you want a ride home?"

I should have said no. I know I did, somewhere in my head. That version of me — the one who makes smart decisions, who keeps things professional — she said no. She probably even meant it.

But that's not what happened.

Instead, I nodded. Small, subtle, but it was all the answer he needed. And somehow, without another word, we slipped out together — past the crowd, past the polite noise, and into a different kind of silence entirely.

The kind that buzzed with anticipation.

We got to my apartment building, pulled into the driveway, and didn't move. The engine was still running, headlights casting long shadows on the pavement, but neither of us made the first move to get out. The conversation had turned easy and slow, like a soft jazz tune playing in the background of something unspoken. I laughed at something he said, and he smiled at something I didn't.

Damien parked the car, half-blocking traffic, and I didn't stop him. I didn't want him to move. Sitting there beside him, cocooned in that dim, humming space between our words, I felt warm, flustered in a way that wasn't just from the late summer heat.

Something was happening in me. Something that had been building since the morning. Since the elevator. Since last night, really. I knew I had to leave before I completely unravelled. Before my restraint collapsed entirely. Because I was smitten — heart-thumping, breath-catching, eye-darting smitten — and doing everything in my power to hide it.

I told myself I was doing a good job, keeping cool, not giving too much away. But then again… maybe I wasn't.

A small part of me — rebellious, aching — wanted more. Not everything, but something. Maybe the brush of his hand over mine. Perhaps the way his eyes might linger if I shifted a little closer. But I didn't want to seem too easy. I didn't want to hand over all the mystery.

So I made my move. I told myself I'd said enough. That it was better to leave with something still unsaid than to say too much. I leaned in, kissed him softly on the cheek — impulsively — and immediately regretted it.

It was innocent. Stupid. Sweet. And way too much. Or maybe too little. I didn't know anymore.

I turned my face away, avoiding his eyes, and before he could react, I stepped out of the car and walked straight toward the entrance of my building, trying not to look back. I told myself I did the right thing.

Until I got home.

And realized I had left my phone in his car.

My stomach dropped. My phone — that lifeline, that archive of everything — sitting there in his passenger seat. Sitting with him.

Going back meant facing him again. The same him I'd spent the whole evening resisting. The same him I'd kissed on the cheek, like a confused, hormone-drenched teenager. Going back risked everything I had tried so hard to keep together tonight.

I wanted him — God, I wanted him. But I also wanted to stay in control.

And right now… I wasn't sure I could have both.

So I sat on the edge of my bed, shoes still on, keys still in hand, trying to think clearly. But I was too close to myself to be objective. And the memory of his eyes, his voice, his scent — they were all still clinging to me like heat on skin after the rain.

I needed a plan. I needed space. I needed… him to call me first.

But then again, my phone was in his car.

After several minutes of pacing and overthinking every possible angle, I finally called Damien from my landline — something I hadn't done in years. My voice was calm, but my heart was doing laps in my chest. I asked if I'd left my phone in his car, pretending it was just a casual thought.

After a quick shuffle and the telltale sound of plastic sliding off leather, he confirmed it.

"I'll bring it back," he said easily, like he hadn't just driven ten minutes away. "I was already on the highway, but it's no big deal."

I told him he didn't have to, but I didn't stop him either. Then came the question that made my breath hitch.

"You want me to meet you in the driveway, or… should I come up?"

It was innocent. A practical question.

But it didn't feel innocent. Not to me.

I froze. My instinct screamed driveway. Safer. Neutral. Fast in, fast out.

But somehow, what came out of my mouth was:
"Come up. If you don't mind."

And just like that, I'd invited temptation into my space.

Worse? The apartment was empty. No voices, no noise, no buffer.

And worse, if anyone had come back and seen him in the apartment, that alone could have ruined the safe life I had crafted for myself.

I told myself it was just a phone drop-off. That was all. No big deal. But I also knew the tension between us wasn't exactly subtle. It hadn't been for a while.

I straightened up, tried to fix my hair in the mirror even though I wasn't going anywhere, and opened the main door to wait for him. My heartbeat filled the hallway.

The seconds ticked louder than the silence.

I didn't know what was going to happen — not exactly. But as I waited there, hand still gripping the doorframe, I could feel something electric stirring in the air.

I wasn't sure if Damien was going to bring the phone, bring his bravado…or bring everything I'd been trying to resist.

But I stayed put, heart pounding, lips pressed together, eyes trained on the elevator.

And waited for the beep of the elevator to scream his arrival. I panicked and thought waiting at the door might seem too eager, so I went back inside the apartment.

My heart sank the moment I heard the knock.

It wasn't fear that gripped me—it was anticipation, thick and pulsing, pressing against my chest like a second heartbeat. I stood frozen, caught in that suspended moment between restraint and surrender. Between turning back and giving in.

Another knock, firmer this time. Like he knew exactly what he was doing to me.

"Coming," I called out, though the word barely left my lips. But maybe he didn't need to hear it. Perhaps he heard everything I couldn't bring myself to say, because the door creaked open anyway.

And there he was.

One foot inside my world, holding my phone like a peace offering—but his eyes, they were the real confession. Dark, hungry, lit with a fire that mirrored the one scorching its way down my spine. I didn't even try to think. Thinking was a luxury for people who hadn't been touched like I'd been touched, kissed like I'd been kissed.

I crossed the room in three breathless steps and launched myself at him. My arms wrapped around his neck as my lips collided with his—not gently, not sweetly, but with the raw ache of everything I'd been holding in since the moment he walked away earlier. It was a kiss that tasted like a question and an answer all at once. A need made flesh.

He responded as if I were his oxygen. One hand gripped my waist, the other slid into my hair, tilting my head so he could kiss me deeper, messier. His fingers dug into my hips, like he wanted to memorize the curve of my body from the outside in. I arched into him, heat blooming between us, and I tugged at his collar until he groaned into my mouth.

There was nothing polite about this. Nothing clean or careful.

This was a collision—of mouths, of limbs, of every second of silence between us finally unravelling. He pressed me up against the wall, the door slamming shut behind him with the finality of a decision we'd already made.

And still, his hands moved—under my shirt, across my stomach, fingers tracing the line of my spine like he was trying to open me one shiver at a time. I gasped into his mouth, and he swallowed it whole. His hips rolled into mine with intention, and I could feel his pulsating need —hard, hot, restrained only by the fabric separating us.

My hands slipped under his shirt, nails dragging across his back, claiming him in return. The groan that rumbled from his chest lit a fire low in my belly. He lifted me in one swift motion, my legs wrapping around him like instinct, and carried me to the nearest surface—an entryway table that trembled under the weight of us both.

He didn't ask. He didn't need to. Every movement was permission, every kiss a promise.

There was no more pretending.

Only this: the heat, the ache, the breathless fall into something too big for either of us to name.

And God, I wanted to fall all the way.

His forehead rested against mine for a beat, both of us breathing hard. His fingers splayed across my lower back, anchoring me in place while his hips stayed pressed firmly between mine. Every inch of contact sent sparks ricocheting through my body.

Neither of us moved.

We just hovered there—our bodies caught in that narrow space between restraint and ruin. His breath was hot against my lips, his fingers twitching like he was trying to hold back, like taking his time was somehow harder than giving in.

My eyes fluttered open to find his already watching me. Intense. Devouring. Like I was the only thing he could see, like I was the answer to some question he didn't even know he'd been asking.

I rolled my hips, just enough to tease him. A test. A spark. He hissed through his teeth and pressed his forehead harder to mine.

"Don't," he said low, like a warning and a plea all at once. "Not unless you want me to lose the last thread of control I've got left."

That was the moment everything stilled. The air thickened, the silence pressed in, but it wasn't empty—it was loaded. Like the moment right before lightning splits the sky.

And in that pause, I realized I didn't just want the storm.

I needed it.

But for now, we just stayed there—frozen in heat, humming with everything that hadn't happened yet, hearts pounding against each other like a rhythm only we knew.

The rest could wait... just a moment longer.

His mouth crashed into mine again—no hesitation this time, no restraint. The thread had snapped. Control was gone, and in its place was a need so overwhelming it blurred everything else out.

He backed me up until my spine met the wall, his hands everywhere—gripping, claiming, moving like they couldn't decide where to settle because they needed all of me at once. His mouth left a trail down my neck, grazing my collarbone before finding the pulse thudding at my throat. He kissed it, then bit down—just enough to make me gasp, to make my knees buckle.

I wrapped my leg around his waist instinctively, and he caught it, hoisting me up with a growl against my skin. I wrapped the other around him as he lifted me fully, pressing me into the wall, holding me there like I weighed nothing at all.

And then he was inside me.

I cried out—loud, involuntarily, raw.

It was sudden and deep, the stretch shocking in the best way. I clung to him as he rocked into me, hard and slow, every thrust deliberate. Like he was carving himself into me, deeper with each movement. My back arched against the wall, my body helpless in his grip, entirely at his mercy—and I loved it. I needed it.

"Damien…" I breathed, but it came out broken, needy, almost a prayer.

His mouth was on mine again, swallowing every moan, every cry, and his hips set a punishing rhythm that made coherent thought impossible. My nails dug into his shoulders, anchoring myself to something as my body trembled with every impact. He was relentless— grinding, thrusting, burying himself over and over as if he wanted to brand the feeling into both of us.

"God, you feel…" he growled, voice ragged, barely human. "So fucking perfect. You're mine. Say it."

"I'm yours," I gasped before I even realized the words were leaving me.

And I meant them. In that moment, in that heat, with his hands holding me like I was something sacred and sinful all at once, I meant every syllable.

The pressure inside me built fast, rising with every wet, perfect connection of our bodies. His mouth never stopped—kissing, biting, worshipping, claiming. Each movement, each sound from him drew me closer to the edge until I shattered in his arms—eyes wide, mouth open in a silent scream, muscles clenching around him like my body was trying to pull him deeper.

With the current coursing through me, he kept thrusting and sending me to a place I never imagined. The orgasm felt like it lasted forever.

He slowed down as I savoured the moment, and the kiss, oh the kiss. It made everything sweeter, like my sexuality had been reborn.

We stayed like that for a moment—fused, trembling, his breath hot against my skin, mine still catching in stutters.

There were no words.

None needed.

Just the sound of our heartbeats colliding and the slow return of reality as the storm began to pass.

He held me there, pressed against the wall, our bodies still locked, his arms like a cage—but not to trap me. To protect. To savour. I felt the way his chest rose and fell against mine, how his breath fanned over my cheek, still uneven, still burning.

His hands slid down slowly, almost reverently, cupping the underside of my thighs before loosening his grip just enough to ease me down. My legs wobbled when my feet touched the ground, and he caught me, one hand steadying my back, the other tracing a path down my side. Every touch was slower now, but no less intense— like he was learning me all over again, this time without urgency, just desire.

I leaned into him, skin slick and sensitive, lips finding his neck as I kissed up to his jaw. He growled low, that sound that always lit me up, and tilted my chin so our mouths could meet again. This kiss was different. Slower. Messier. Hot and open-mouthed, with tongues dancing and teeth grazing. Still hungry. Still desperate.

He turned me around, walking me backward toward the couch without breaking the kiss. When we reached it, he sank onto the cushions and pulled me onto his lap, my knees bracketing his hips. I felt him still thick and hard beneath me, and a shiver rolled down my spine.

"You sure?" he murmured, lips brushing my ear.

I nodded, but he didn't take my word for it. His hands explored me again, caressing, testing, coaxing soft moans from my throat until he was sure I wasn't just ready, but begging.

When I finally sank onto him again, both of us gasped in unison.

It was slower this time. Deeper. The kind of rhythm that made me feel every inch of him, every shift, every twitch. His hands gripped my hips, guiding me, while my fingers tangled in his hair, my head falling back as waves of sensation pulsed through me.

He filled me so completely, it felt like our bodies were built for this—like we weren't just fucking, we were syncing. The tension wound tight again, a new crescendo rising, and I rode it with him, rolling my hips, matching his every move until our breaths were wild and tangled again.

"You're incredible," he whispered, eyes locked on mine. "So fucking beautiful like this."

I clenched around him at his words, and he felt it, his head falling back with a low curse.

The climb was slower, but the fall was just as devastating. When I came again, it rolled through me like thunder, and he held me as my body shook, hips still moving until his release took him over, gripping me tight, body pulsing beneath mine.

After that, we stayed tangled together. Skin on skin. Heartbeats thumping in sync. His arms wrapped around me like he never wanted to let go. I laid my head on his shoulder, breathing slowly, evening out, our sweat cooling between us.

It was raw. It was tender. It was everything.

And for the first time in a long time, I didn't care where we went next.

I just knew I didn't want to leave his arms.

Silence settled over the room—not heavy, not awkward, but full. Like our bodies had used up the air, and we were just now remembering how to breathe. I laid on the couch, my chest still rising and falling, heart still racing but for a different reason now.

I stared at the ceiling, at nothing, really. It was quiet, but my thoughts were deafening.

What just happened?

I could still feel him beside me, the warmth of his skin brushing mine, his fingers tracing idle patterns across my thigh like he couldn't stop touching me. A part of me wanted to pull away, to pretend I wasn't this swept up, this open. But the bigger part of me... didn't move. It didn't want to.

I was scared. Not of him—but of myself. Of how quickly I gave in. How badly I'd wanted it. How good it had felt not to overthink, to just feel. I couldn't remember the last time I let go like that. The last time someone looked at me like I wasn't just someone they were with, but someone they were completely drawn to.

It was thrilling. Terrifying.

I wasn't sure what I wanted from him beyond this moment, but I knew something had shifted. This wasn't just a casual thing, not anymore. At least not to me. And that realization came with a knot in my stomach.

What was I doing?

I turned slightly, just enough to glimpse him in the low light—hair a mess, lips still parted like he wanted to say something but didn't know how.

This was dangerous territory, and I didn't trust myself not to fall too far, too fast.

Still… my body was humming. My heart was quiet now, but it beat a little differently.

And as he pulled me close without a word, like it was the most natural thing in the world, I realized—I wasn't ready to let go just yet.

I rolled over, trying to gather my thoughts before they unravelled completely. My hair was a mess, my cheeks still warm, and I was suddenly hyper-aware of the silence. He looked at me like he was waiting—for a cue, a word, something. I couldn't bring myself to say, "You should go," and I definitely wasn't ready to explain why he shouldn't stay. Not yet. Maybe not ever.

So instead, I said, "Let's go back to the hotel."

I watched his eyebrows lift just slightly, and his crooked grin made a quiet appearance. I could tell what he was thinking—probably thought it was a sign I was getting hooked. And maybe I was. But I couldn't have him lingering here, in this space that held too much of my life. He didn't know who I lived with, and I wasn't about to explain why that mattered. I didn't want to lie, but I wasn't ready to let him into that part of my world yet, either.

"Just easier," I added, brushing a piece of hair behind my ear, pretending it was no big deal. "You're heading back there anyway."

He nodded, playing it cool, but I could tell his ego was satisfied. A woman asking to come with him? That was a power trip for most men. For him, it probably felt like a clean victory. But he didn't press. He let me have my reasoning.

I gathered a few things, threw on something comfortable but presentable, and stuffed the rest into my bag without looking at him too much. I opened the windows, quickly tidied up, and we left the apartment with a kind of hush hanging in the air. Not awkward, just... unsure. Like neither of us quite knew what this meant now that the line between attraction and intimacy had disappeared entirely.

He opened the car door for me—unnecessary, but sweet. And as I slid into the seat, I realized I wasn't nervous anymore.

I was curious.

Curious about how long I could keep this going without it spiralling. Curious about whether he saw this as just a detour or something more. I was also curious about myself—this version of me that was breaking all her rules.

And as we pulled away from the curb, I didn't look back at the apartment.

I wasn't sure if that was a good thing or not.

Dancing with Fire

We got back to the hotel, both pretending like we weren't holding the weight of what had just happened between us. Instead of heading straight to the room, we found ourselves at the bar—dim lighting, hushed jazz, the soft clink of glasses around us. It was oddly comforting, the way the world around us slowed down just enough for us to sit shoulder to shoulder without the pressure of closed doors and unspoken expectations.

We ordered drinks, something simple. I didn't need courage or excuses. I just wanted the quiet hum of a shared moment. Damien had this way of slipping into conversation that made it easy to forget how complicated everything had suddenly become. He talked about work, about the politics behind the latest executive shuffle, and I let myself lean into it. We dissected the industry with the honesty of people who'd stopped trying to impress each other. He cursed about a particular partner's incompetence, and I laughed—not the polite kind, but the real kind that bubbled from somewhere unguarded.

And maybe that's what steadied me.

Because while I was with him, I wasn't craving him in that aching, desperate way I had earlier. It was like he'd already given my body what it needed. The tension that had gripped me all day had finally found release, and now I could breathe—deeply, even breaths that didn't shudder with want.

Still, he looked good in this light. Too good. His sleeves rolled up, collar slightly undone, a small smirk resting at the corner of his lips every time I said something that surprised him. There was a little dance in the way he listened—like he liked peeling back the layers I'd kept hidden from everyone else.

I sipped slowly, letting the alcohol warm my throat but not dull my thoughts. I watched the way he leaned closer when I spoke, the occasional brush of his arm against mine feeling more like punctuation than an accident. Every touch was light, casual—but it landed heavy. A reminder. A promise.

We didn't talk about what happened earlier. Not directly. But it was there in the way his eyes lingered a little too long on my lips, in the way my foot accidentally pressed against his under the table and didn't move right away. We were speaking around it, building a fortress of words so we didn't have to look directly at the fire still smouldering beneath the surface.

And yet, I liked it. I liked that we could be two things at once—raw and refined. Tense and at ease. Laughing in a quiet hotel bar like we hadn't just tangled up our bodies and left reason on the living room floor.

I wasn't sure where the night was going. But I knew I didn't want it to end.

I excused myself to freshen up—a simple thing, a pause to breathe, to collect myself. I told myself I needed to fix my hair, touch up my lipstick, maybe just take a minute away from the magnetic pull that was him. But in truth, I was trying to buy time from my own unravelling.

When I returned, the sight stopped me cold. He was standing near the bar, leaning just slightly into conversation with two women—smartly dressed, confident, laughing a little too freely. One touched his arm as she said something. The other tilted her head with that interested gleam women have when they think they've found someone worth pursuing.

And just like that, the fire I thought he'd put out earlier came roaring back to life.

Jealousy wasn't an emotion I was used to. It rose hot and fast, bitter like adrenaline. My chest tightened. My steps faltered. I felt suddenly foolish—like a little girl dressing up in adult emotions, playing at control I didn't have. My stomach knotted, and before I could even check myself, I walked over and said I was leaving.

I didn't explain. I didn't wait for a response.

Maybe I wanted to pull his attention back. Maybe I was punishing him for something he hadn't even done. Or maybe—I was punishing myself.

Because none of this was like me.

I'd always taken pride in being strong. Unshakable. Practical. I never leaned too hard on anyone. I never played coy or let myself be "that" girl—the one who flinched at attention being divided, the one who let herself spiral over something as unspoken as a glance. But there I was, feeling my composure melt away like sugar under a flame.

Something about him stripped me of all my careful armour.

He hadn't promised me anything. He hadn't said the words. But the way he had touched me... the way his hands had learned my body like it was something he was born to know... the way he listened when I spoke and looked at me like he saw right through me—it was enough to wreck all the lines I'd drawn for myself.

I hated that. And I loved it.

I hated how weak it made me feel. But God, how beautiful it felt to surrender.

Every time I tried to pull back, I only fell harder. Like trying to climb out of water only to realize you'd already sunk too deep. I kept reaching for air, for distance, for control—but the truth was, I didn't want any of it. Not really. I wanted him. Not just his body, but the strange safety he gave me in a world where I never allowed myself to be soft.

The more I tried to fight it, the more I fractured. And piece by piece, I was falling for him. Not gracefully, not with poetic logic—but hard, messy, and unprepared.

And I didn't know what scared me more: how much I wanted him... or how much I might already need him.

I walked towards the exit, and he followed me without saying anything.

We left the hotel without saying much. Not because there wasn't anything to say, but because the silence between us had grown comfortable—charged, but not heavy. I didn't want to go home. Not yet. And definitely not alone. But I also didn't want him thinking I was some smitten schoolgirl chasing something more than what we had. I was toeing a delicate line—between wanting to be with him and wanting to appear untouched by him.

We walked aimlessly at first, not even discussing where we were going. The city was winding down around us— its buzz softening into a hum. Streetlights flickered. Distant music spilled from a rooftop bar. I caught glimpses of us in reflective storefronts, walking side by side, our pace synced like we'd been doing this for years. There was something soothing about it, almost surreal. My heart wasn't pounding the way it had earlier, but it was beating differently—steadier, warmer.

A few times, I caught myself wanting to reach out, to brush my fingers against his or loop my arm through his. I just want to feel his weight beside me, to make it real in a more public, quiet way. But I pulled back every time. Holding his hand would've said too much. Or maybe it would've said exactly what I felt—and that was the danger.

The garage loomed ahead, our steps echoing against the concrete walls as we approached the car. It wasn't far, but I wished the walk was longer. I didn't want the moment to end. I didn't want the spell to break. Being next to him like this, doing nothing spectacular, felt... real. Not lust-driven. Not charged. Just us—in a calm I didn't know I'd been craving.

And still, every time our arms brushed, every time he looked at me with that unreadable softness in his eyes, I wondered if he knew. If he could feel the storm beneath my calm.

I had spent years building a fortress around my emotions. Strong. Independent. Composed. And yet here I was—thinking about how not holding his hand might be the most effort I'd put into self-control all year.

Because if I did... if I reached for him and he held on... I may never want to let go.

As we neared his car, the shift in atmosphere was immediate. The air was different in the garage—denser, quieter, laced with the hum of distant engines and our footsteps echoing off cold concrete walls. It was the kind of silence that makes you feel things louder. And that's when it hit me... again.

The quiet stirred something inside me. It wasn't a thought, not something I could name with words—it was more like a voice. Urgent. Breathless. Screaming for me to do something. To feel something. To act.

That stillness, that masked calm of the garage, somehow made everything hotter. More dangerous. More... magnetic. We'd been in a lounge with dim lights and other people just minutes ago. I had been collected, composed, sipping from a glass and pretending I wasn't thinking about what his hands felt like. But here? With only him, and no audience, no interruptions, no pretense?

The shift was seismic.

My breath hitched ever so slightly, and I prayed he didn't notice. My heart had picked up pace like it knew the rhythm of where this was heading, and honestly, elsewhere was pounding just as hard.

I walked like nothing was wrong. Like I hadn't just unravelled at the seams internally. I stayed cool on the outside, but inside, my body was on fire. I wanted his hands on me. Everywhere. I wanted to feel the heat of his breath on my neck, the press of his chest against my back, the weight of him pinning me to some cool metal surface. The thought alone made my knees tremble beneath my steady stride.

I didn't know what scared me more—how badly I wanted him… or how badly I didn't care anymore about hiding it.

We reached the car, and he looked at me with a quiet smile. I met his eyes, just briefly. But that look—that look—was enough to set my body ablaze all over again.

I wanted to say something. Anything. But the only voice loud now was the one inside me, whispering with reckless urgency:
"Do it. Take it. This moment will never come again."

He moved toward the passenger side, ever the gentleman, reaching to open the door for me.

But I couldn't. Not this time.

I stepped forward, grabbed the door, and shut it with a soft but deliberate click.

He turned, surprised, brows lifted—maybe to ask what was wrong.

But I didn't let him get a word out.

I pushed him back, hard enough for his back to press against the cool metal of the car. The clang echoed in the stillness of the garage. His eyes widened just slightly, but not in protest—in something far more dangerous.

Before he could speak, I crushed my lips against his. There was no preamble, no subtlety—just heat. Raw and reckless. The kiss was messy, hungry, and absolutely unplanned. My hands tangled in his collar as I pressed my body into him, needing to feel every inch. There was no more hiding, no space left for restraint. This was me… taking.

He gasped slightly into my mouth, caught between the kiss and the shock of it. But he didn't stop me. His hands found my waist, then my hips, then slid lower, pulling me closer like the risk only made it hotter. And maybe it did—perhaps it made everything more intoxicating. I could feel his body tightening beneath mine, could feel his control slipping.

We both knew it was stupid. We both knew there were probably cameras in the garage. The wrong person walking by, the wrong frame caught on film—and my name would be dragged through the dirt alongside his. "Senior Partner caught in heated moment with... someone who should've known better."

But still—I didn't stop.

Because in that moment, I wasn't thinking about my firm or what anyone would say. I wasn't thinking about professionalism, about titles, or about what this would mean on Monday morning. I was thinking about how right it felt to finally stop pretending. About how badly I needed his hands on me again.

I broke the kiss just long enough to catch my breath, resting my forehead against his, my chest heaving. He didn't say anything. His fingers gripped my hips tightly, and the way he looked at me—hungry, conflicted, amazed—made it even harder to walk away.

I whispered, almost without meaning to, "Tell me to stop... or take me back upstairs."

His jaw clenched slightly. His pupils dilated.

And that's when I knew—I wasn't the only one losing control tonight.

His hands slid to my waist—firm, commanding, but with a searching quality that betrayed his restraint. Like he wasn't just touching me—he was confirming I was really there, that this moment wasn't some fantasy we'd both secretly indulged too many times. His fingers gripped tighter as though anchoring himself, and I could feel the pulse of his want through every inch of his skin. It matched mine. Raw. Electric.

Then he paused—just a breath, just a moment—and pulled away enough to glance around. His eyes were sharp, assessing, scanning the garage like a man who wanted to lose control but couldn't afford the consequences. That flicker of awareness—of risk—only made it hotter. I didn't know what he saw, and I didn't care. When he took my hand, his grip was urgent, silent, full of intent. He led me toward a shadowed corner, tucked between concrete columns and crates that smelled faintly of dust and metal.

The moment we stopped, the space between us snapped like a rubber band pulled too tight for too long. The air was heavy, alive, pulsing with energy that wrapped around us like static. I could feel it in my throat, in my spine, between my thighs. I reached for him without thinking, and my fingers found his zipper. They shook—not from fear, but from the sheer gravity of this release. Of hours of tension now begging for reckoning.

As the zipper slid down, time seemed to slow. My breath hitched, chest rising and falling against him, and the sound of fabric shifting in the stillness was deafening. I didn't look up—I couldn't. My focus was singular, primal. But he moved too, just as sure. His hands swept beneath my skirt, finding skin with a hunger that bordered on reverence. And then his mouth. God—his mouth. It trailed along my collarbone, then lower, finding that tender place at the base of my neck, the spot that made my knees threaten to give out.

My skin was on fire. My spine arched. And every touch he gave me lit another fuse.

By the time his lips brushed against the inside of my thigh, my body was no longer mine. I was trembling, not from the cold, but from an unbearable need to feel more. Every breath I took felt like it might be the one that shattered me. When his tongue met me there, I had to bite down on my lip so hard I tasted blood. I wanted to scream. I wanted to let the whole garage know what he was doing to me. But I couldn't—not here, not now. So my body spoke for me in every tremor, every clenched fist, every breathless gasp I tried to swallow.

And then he stood, meeting my eyes with a look that said nothing and everything all at once. In a single, fluid motion, he lifted me. My back pressed to the cold wall, the sharp chill a perfect contrast to the heat blooming between us. He slid inside me, and my entire world narrowed to that moment. That movement. That burn of pressure and need and pleasure.

Each thrust wasn't just physical—it was a confession. A possession. Every drive of his hips stripped something off me—doubt, pride, control—until I was bare and aching and only his. My fingers dug into his shoulders, trying to hold on, but it was futile. I was falling. Every breath was a cry I couldn't voice. Every moan was a war with silence I kept losing. My legs trembled around him, my core tightening with every delicious thrust.

And when he turned me, bent me forward, and pressed himself into me again, I surrendered entirely. There was no part of me that wasn't begging for this. For him. For the complete collapse of whatever armour I had left.

When I came, it wasn't soft. It was a storm. A full-body convulsion that pulled a sound from my throat I barely managed to muffle against my arm. He followed, and for the first time, I heard him let go—truly let go—with a grunt that felt like it came from somewhere deep in his chest. It was the sexiest thing I'd ever heard. Honest. Unapologetic. Wild.

In that moment, under the buzz of overhead fluorescents and the threat of discovery, we didn't just give in—we gave up. Gave ourselves.

And I had never felt more dangerously alive in my entire life.

We collapsed to the ground, breathless and spent, our bodies tangled in the aftermath of something that had felt too big to contain in flesh and skin. The concrete was cool beneath us, grounding us, shocking against the fever still coursing through my limbs. My heart was still pounding in my ears, louder than it had any right to be —until I heard something else.

A sound.

Voices. Maybe footsteps. Distant, but moving—closer or away, I couldn't tell. All I knew was that for a split second, the spell cracked. Damien's head snapped up, and without a word, instinct took over. He was on his feet in one breath, and in the next, his hand was under my arm, strong and urgent, lifting me up like I weighed nothing. My legs were jelly, but I moved on sheer will—driven by the same thrill that had pulled me into him minutes ago.

We didn't speak as we slipped out through the stairwell. Just the thud of our feet echoing against the metal steps and the frantic rhythm of our breath bouncing off the walls. We didn't look back. We didn't need to. Everything that mattered had already happened.

And God, what had just happened?

I felt like a teenager again. Reckless. Free. Touched in places I hadn't even known existed inside me. The kind of touch that doesn't just skim your skin—it sinks into your bones and rewrites something fundamental. My body still ached with the memory of him inside me, the ghost of his breath still tingling on my skin. I could still feel the press of his hand over my mouth, the wildness of it all—how close we had come to being caught, how close I had come to falling apart completely.

It wasn't just sex. It was release. It was a need, poured out in the most desperate, dangerous way. Nothing in my life—no hook-up, no lover, no whispered promise in the dark—had ever touched me like that. Ever made me lose myself so fully. Nothing had ever peeled me open and reached into the quiet corners I'd sealed off so long ago.

And yes, maybe there were cameras. Perhaps someone had heard us. Maybe this could cost me everything I'd worked so damn hard for.

But in that moment, I didn't care.

I wasn't thinking about consequences for the first time in what felt like forever. I wasn't measuring the weight of my actions or calculating how to fold this back into the neat lines of my life. I was just… feeling. Raw, wild, and utterly alive.

And I wasn't sure if I was terrified—or ready to let the whole thing burn.

Poisoned by Desire

He offered—because, of course, he did. Always the gentleman, even now. "Let me take you home," he said, voice soft and steady, the kind of steady that was anything but calm. That voice... it did something to me. Turned simple phrases into sin.

But I didn't want safe. I didn't want an ending. I wanted more.

"No," I said quietly, eyes locking with his. "Take me back to your hotel."

There was a pause. Barely half a second. But I felt it. Saw it. That flicker in his gaze, like something ancient and raw, had just awakened. Not shock. Not even surprise. Just... recognition. Like he'd been hoping I'd say it, but didn't dare assume. Like he already knew we'd reached the point of no return, and this was just the moment we both finally stopped pretending.

He didn't speak. Just nodded once and turned, leading the way.

We left the garage without a word, but the silence between us wasn't empty—it was charged. Our footsteps echoed against the quiet night, but everything else—the rhythm of our breathing, the swing of my hips just a little more exaggerated, the way his fingers curled and flexed at his sides—was loud in all the ways that mattered.

The air had shifted.

His jacket brushed mine as we walked side by side, too close not to touch but still holding that sliver of restraint between us. Every part of me buzzed with it. The ache hadn't faded—it had deepened. Slowed into something heavier, deeper, more dangerous.

A few people passed us on the sidewalk. I barely noticed. I was aware only of him—his heat, his scent, the way his eyes glanced down at my mouth when he thought I wasn't looking. The way he seemed to move slower now, like drawing out the walk was its own form of foreplay.

When we stepped into the lobby, the light hit us differently. I felt bare, exposed, like the woman beside him wasn't the one who had walked into that garage but someone new. Someone stripped down to her want, her hunger, her truth.

He pressed the elevator button, and I could feel his pulse even though we weren't touching. My heart was drumming so loudly, I was sure the sound would give me away.

Still, we said nothing.

But when the elevator doors opened and he reached for my hand—finally, deliberately—I didn't hesitate.

I let him lead me in, fingers laced tight in his, and as the doors slid shut behind us, sealing the two of us inside that mirrored box, I exhaled.

Not in relief.

In surrender.

Because whatever this was, wherever it was going, I was already his.

And I had no desire—no ability—to stop it now.

The moment the doors slid shut, I turned to him—my body moving before my mind had time to second-guess. I kissed him—deep, consuming—not to seduce, not to provoke, but to brand him. A reminder. A promise. A whisper that said: I'm still on fire for you.

He didn't say a word. He didn't have to. His hands grazed my waist, but barely. As if he were holding back, as if he knew that if he gave in here, in this confined space of steel and glass, we'd never make it to the room.

When we reached his floor and stepped out, my steps were quiet but deliberate, his just behind mine—close enough to feel, not close enough to touch. I was still floating from the parking lot, from that reckless, glorious high that had stripped me bare in every way. But I wasn't done. I didn't want to come down. Not yet.

The door clicked open, and I walked in ahead of him. He had barely set down his keycard when I turned, pushed him back onto the bed with a steady hand on his chest, and climbed onto him without hesitation. The look on his face was pure astonishment—eyes wide, pupils dark, lips parted. He hadn't seen this version of me. Hell, I hadn't seen this version of me.

But tonight, I was the storm. I was the director of this moment, and he was my audience—captive, breathless, beautifully undone.

I stood at the foot of the bed and began to undress, slowly. Not seductively for the sake of performance, but with a quiet power that came from knowing exactly what he wanted—and how deeply I was willing to give it to him. One piece at a time. My jacket, tossed over the chair. My blouse, unbuttoned with aching patience. Each reveal was matched with a walk to the bed—where I knelt over him and took something from him too. First, his belt. Then his shirt. Then his pants. A trade of power wrapped in silk and tension.

His breathing deepened. I could see the way his chest rose and fell, the way his fingers gripped the edge of the sheets like he was trying to ground himself. His eyes never left me, not even for a second. Not when I unhooked my bra. Not when my panties slid to the floor. Not when I stepped closer, wearing nothing but the heat between us and the need we had both been denying for too long.

By the time I stood before him, bare and unflinching, he was trembling with restraint.

And I? I had never felt more in control.

I stood before him, nothing clung to me but the curl of my smile and the weight of his gaze. The air between us had shifted—no longer playful, no longer restrained. It was charged, magnetic, almost dangerous in its heat.

I lifted one knee onto the bed—slow, intentional—then the other, the cool sheets brushing up against my skin in soft contrast to the fire rising inside me. His eyes tracked every movement like he didn't just want me—he needed me. Elbows braced behind him, muscles taut beneath his skin, he looked like a man on the edge of unravelling.

I moved toward him on all fours—slow, fluid, unhurried. A lioness, not hunting, but claiming. Owning. My gaze never wavered from his, and the tension crackled louder with every inch I closed.

But just as I reached him, just when his breath hitched and I felt the shift in his body, ready to meet mine, I stopped. I tilted my head, let a smirk dance on my lips, and watched the flicker in his expression change. Confusion. Realization. And then—fire. His eyes darkened with the weight of understanding.

Without a word, I lowered myself—not to tease, not to test—but to worship. My hands gripped his thighs with slow control, grounding him, guiding him. And when my mouth found him, warm and wanting, his breath caught like he'd been sucker punched by pleasure. The kind of gasp that held his whole chest in it.

His fingers fisted in the sheets—white-knuckled restraint —as I worked him with the kind of devotion that didn't come from duty, but from desire. From hours of holding back. From knowing exactly what kind of storm we had been dancing around and finally choosing to step into the centre of it.

Every movement of my tongue was deliberate. Not rushed, not frenzied—just deep, slow precision meant to draw him out, inch by inch. He groaned, low and guttural, the sound vibrating straight through my core and making my thighs press together without thinking.

This wasn't just physical.

It was communion.

A moment that hummed with power—mine, for now— but given freely. And with every shift of his hips, every breathless curse that fell from his lips, I knew:

I wasn't breaking him. I was freeing him.

And I was nowhere near done.

I could taste just how much he wanted me—every slow, deliberate lick drawing a new wave of tension from his body, a symphony of urgency building beneath my tongue. His grip on the sheets tightened until his knuckles turned white, every ragged breath he released threaded with those deep, guttural sounds that made my insides coil tighter with satisfaction.

I wasn't just touching him—I was reading him. Learning him in a language more intimate than speech, translating every subtle twitch, every faltering inhale, every muscle gone rigid under my hands. The rest of him blurred—his chest, his arms, even the quiet fire still smouldering in his eyes. None of it mattered. Not in this moment. There was only this—the heat that pulsed against my lips, the core of his hunger, the part of him that had already brought me to the edge in some hidden corner of a garage wall and left me wanting more.

This wasn't just pleasure.

It was reverence.

A tribute carved from the ruins of restraint. A thank-you whispered in flicks of my tongue, in the relentless pace I held—not cruel, but unwavering. I was offering myself not in apology, but in recognition—for how completely he'd undone me, and how I'd let him.

And when I slowed, just enough to tease—pulling back, circling, drawing delicate little tremors out of him like strings from an instrument he didn't know he was playing—he responded with beautiful instinct. His hips jerked up, then held back, the discipline in him starting to crack under the weight of it all.

That tension? Exquisite.

But what came next—that was everything.

A sound, raw and deeper than the first he gave me back in the garage, ripped out of him like something primal had broken loose. His body surged and stilled all at once, release crashing into him in a way that felt cosmic, inevitable. And I stayed there, wrapped around him, collecting every shudder, every low groan that spilled from him like confessions.

Only when I felt the last tremor fade did I finally lift my head, slow and steady, letting the air fill again with breath and knowing.

I wiped the corner of my mouth with the back of my hand, his taste still lingering like a secret I'd never tell. Then I met his gaze with a smirk that didn't ask for validation—it declared it.

Message delivered.

Message received.

Game, very much on.

I leaned in and kissed him—soft this time. Not with hunger, not with heat, but something gentler. Something real. A quiet adoration that said I'm here, not I want. It was the first breath of stillness after a night thick with urgency, the kind of kiss that lands not just on skin but somewhere deeper—beneath all the noise, all the need.

Then I settled beside him, bodies flush, hearts still racing but no longer sprinting. His arm wrapped around me like it belonged there. Like I did. And I let myself melt into him, no hesitation. No second-guessing. Just that rare, aching relief of feeling safe—not just in body, but in spirit. As if the pieces I kept trying to hold together had finally found their place. Their person.

His fingers traced slow, wandering lines over my skin, lazy and affectionate, like he was learning me in silence. Memorizing me. I mirrored the motion—my hand sweeping over his chest, his shoulder, down the curve of his arm, each inch an unspoken vow: I see you. I'm still here.

We didn't talk. We didn't need to.

We had already said everything in other ways—through hands, mouths, and tension so loud it felt like screaming. Now came the quiet aftermath, the sacred kind. Not the absence of desire, but the echo of something more profound. A peace we hadn't expected. A stillness we hadn't earned—but found anyway.

I curled closer, listening to the cadence of his breath. Wondering if he felt it too—that shift. That trembling calm. That strange and beautiful moment when lust softens, deepens, and becomes something else entirely. Presence. Realness. That terrifyingly tender thing that sneaks in when the armour's down.

And wrapped in his warmth, I finally let go of the last piece of resistance I didn't even know I was still holding.

Time passed—not measured, just felt—until he looked at me. Really looked. The kind of gaze that doesn't just meet yours, but reaches past it. His eyes searched not just for the woman in front of him, but for the woman behind all the defences. And in that look, I saw a question I couldn't name. And an answer I wasn't ready to say.

Then he kissed me.

And this time, it was his softness. His intention. His way of saying I feel it too. It wasn't rushed. It didn't need to be. It tasted like honey, heat, and something dangerously close to love—and that terrified me more than anything. But I kissed him back. Fully. Willingly. Because I was already too far in to lie to myself now.

But the kiss... the kiss was only the prelude.

Because the moment his tongue met mine, my body betrayed me. A low, hungry ache surged to the surface, and I couldn't hold it back. He didn't need direction. He never did. His hands were already moving—gliding over my hips, my waist, every curve like he was charting sacred territory. And when his lips broke from mine and drifted to my neck, I felt the breath catch in my throat.

His tongue traced along the delicate skin there—slow, hot, purposeful. His breath fanned out in waves. My pulse went wild, my back arched, and I was gone again, undone by the simplicity of how I felt seen under every kiss.

He took his time down my body, mouth reverent, touch steady. When he reached my breasts, he paused—not just to admire, but to savour. Kissing them like they were soft altars meant to be worshipped. Not rushed. Not claimed. Just honoured.

But we both knew where he was going. And I didn't shy away. I welcomed it. Welcomed him. Opened myself—physically, emotionally, completely.

The moment his tongue found its place—found me—it was electric. I arched instinctively, my fingers clawing into the sheets, a gasp slipping from my lips before I could catch it. It was too much and somehow still not enough. My body was already tipping, teetering on the edge of something seismic, but I knew him. Knew his rhythm, his patience, that infuriating and beautiful precision. He wasn't here to rush me toward pleasure.

He was here to unmake me, one slow stroke of his delicious tongue at a time.

His hands cradled my hips with that quiet reverence only he seemed capable of—steady, warm, firm. Not just holding me, but grounding me. Guiding me through a storm I didn't even know I'd summoned. Every flick of his tongue was a poetic verse written in heat and tension. My body answered him in kind, hips lifting, muscles trembling, a moan caught at the back of my throat.

And still, he didn't let me go. Not yet.

It was maddening, the way he kept pulling me back just as I got close—teasing, softening, tracing the edges of pleasure like he wanted to memorize every contour of my ache. He kissed the inside of my thigh then, slow and tender, like an apology and a promise all at once. I gasped again, chest heaving, the beat of my heart crashing in my ears like a drumline made of need.

And then, he returned.

Slower now. Softer. And something shifted. Not just inside my body, but between us. This wasn't just about sensation. This was intimacy in its rawest form. The kind where someone isn't just chasing your climax—they're studying the way you come undone. And cherishing every second of it.

And I did.

I came undone.

Silently at first—a breath caught, a ripple starting deep and low. Then it swept through me in waves: trembling, gasping, surrendering to the heat. My legs quaked. My back arched. My body ceased to belong to me.

And he stayed with me.

Never letting go. Never flinching. Just holding me with his mouth, his hands, his presence—as if he needed it too. As if he had poured something of himself into me and wanted to witness every echo of it come alive.

When I finally sank into the mattress, limbs loose and lungs searching for air, I blinked up at the ceiling like I had just survived something sacred. And maybe I had. Because this wasn't just about lust. Or want. Or even passion.

This was a kind of worship.

And in his hands, under his mouth, with my name trembling on his breath—I felt holy.

I laid there with my eyes closed, breath still shallow, my body loose and trembling in the quiet aftermath. Every part of me felt spent—like I'd been emptied and filled all at once. His hand moved to my side, warm and steady, tracing slow, languid patterns along the curve of my waist. It was soft—almost reverent. Not the urgency from before, but something gentler. Something healing. His touch grounded me, like he was trying to guide me back from the wild, uncharted place he'd just taken me to.

When I opened my eyes, I didn't feel self-conscious. The layers we wore around others—shyness, fear, performance—were gone. There were no roles left between us. Just two people who had dared to be fully seen. And I knew that something had shifted without him saying a word. Something real. Something deep.

He leaned in and brushed his lips against my temple, his breath warm against my skin. "Are you okay?" he whispered.

It wasn't just about my body—that much I could tell. There was a tremor in his voice, a kind of hesitation that made it clear this question was bigger than just the physical. Do you feel this too? It was the kind of vulnerability that disarms you, not with fragility, but with sincerity.

I nodded, my fingers curling into his chest, not wanting to pull away. "More than okay," I whispered, my voice thick, trembling at the edges. I meant it. More than the pleasure, more than the hunger, it was this—the afterglow wrapped in quiet closeness—that made me feel undone in the best way. "I've never... I've never felt anything like this."

His arm tightened around me, pulling me closer. I could feel his chest rising and falling against mine, our breaths slowly syncing. His hand found mine, fingers intertwining gently, like a silent vow he didn't yet know how to speak aloud.

And even though I felt the weight of what we had just shared, it didn't feel heavy. It felt light. Like the world had tilted slightly, and we had found a new centre—each other. This wasn't just lust. It wasn't just chemistry. It was something quietly anchoring, like a secret neither of us had known we were keeping.

"You're…" he started, then paused, the words catching in his throat. He swallowed, like he needed a second to gather the truth before speaking it. "You're more than I ever expected."

I turned to look at him, really taking in his appearance. And in his eyes, I saw it—this unguarded truth. Like I was the answer to a question he hadn't realized he'd been asking. It made my heart race. Made something inside me stretch open in ways I hadn't expected either.

"More than you expected?" I echoed, trying to tease, but my voice was soft, unsure. Because I hadn't expected this either. I hadn't expected him to feel like this.

He smiled—gentle, raw, honest. "Yeah. More."

And just like that, the air between us shifted again, charged with something fragile and full of promise. We didn't need to define it. We didn't need to know where it was going. All that mattered was that something had happened—was happening—and it felt worth trusting.

I pulled him closer, my lips brushing against his in a soft, lingering kiss. No urgency. No need to chase heat. Just connection. The kind that says I see you. I trust this.

He kissed me back just as gently, his hand cradling my face like I was something precious. And I let him. I let it all in—his touch, his warmth, this terrifying, beautiful thing we were building.

And for the first time, I didn't hold back.

I let myself feel it—entirely, freely.

Without hesitation.

Without fear.

When we finally pulled back, our foreheads rested together, breath mingling in the hush between us. The silence wasn't empty—it was full of everything we weren't saying, everything we had already shared. I could hear my heartbeat in a quiet, steady, and specific way, as if it finally had something to beat for.

Unleashed Passion

I was back to myself that Sunday morning —composed, capable, radiant in my blazer and heels, walking with the measured grace of a woman who owned the room. It was the second and final day of the seminar, and I carried the weight of my title with ease, greeting familiar faces, exchanging pleasantries, and commanding every interaction with quiet confidence. No one would've guessed that just hours earlier, I had been breathless beneath him, losing myself in something far more profound than just physical release.

I had gone home in the early morning light, washed away the scent of our night, and pieced together a lie about where I'd been all night—a lie so smooth it surprised even me. Then I returned to the hotel, as if nothing had happened, wearing professionalism like a second skin. But inside, something was different. Something had been touched, shaken loose. I wasn't the same woman I'd been before the garage... before the hotel room... before him.

And it wasn't until late morning, as I stood laughing lightly with a group of visiting reps, that it happened. A colleague I'd known for years—who knew my quirks, my tells, my moods—smiled and said, "You're glowing today."

That one word. Glowing.

The syllables lingered in the air too long. It hit me like a crash of warm waves against a fragile shore. I froze for a heartbeat too long, and in that stillness, it all came rushing back—the way his hands had held me like I was something sacred, the raw need in his eyes, the way I had screamed into the pillow without shame or apology. I was reliving it. Every touch. Every taste. Every time I begged for more. A simple compliment had cracked open a dam I didn't know I was holding back.

I laughed it off, of course. I said something coy. But inside, I felt exposed—raw, undone. I felt like they could all see through me. Like the glow they noticed wasn't from a good night's sleep or a productive morning... but from being worshipped, from being devoured, from being claimed in ways I hadn't known I needed.

And though I carried on with the rest of the morning, doing my job, speaking on panels, and networking with polished charm, a Pandora's box had been cracked open. And there was no putting those memories, those sensations, that fire... back in.

I excused myself to freshen up, ducking into the quiet sanctuary of the hotel restroom, the click of my heels echoing like a metronome counting down my unravelling. My reflection stared back at me—composed, flawless, poised... but I saw right through it. Beneath the mascara and the carefully applied lip gloss was a woman teetering between her need and her better judgment.

I turned on the tap, letting cold water rush over my trembling hands, trying to let it absorb the heat that still lingered from the memory of his mouth, his hands, and the way he had looked at me, as if I were his and nothing else mattered. But everything did matter. Everything I had built. My name, my role, my image. And he—this—was a threat to all of it.

I knew what was happening. I was aware. Hyper-aware. Too aware. This wasn't just infatuation—it was hunger, dangerous and unrelenting, and I needed to get it under control before it spilled into the one space I could never afford to corrupt: the office.

The next day, we were going back to the real world. No hotel rooms. No elevators humming with anticipation. No dark corners of parking garages. Just glass walls, open desks, board meetings, and paper trails. I had worked too hard, carved my name too cleanly into the space I held there. I couldn't let this follow me back.

But it wasn't that simple. Because I needed him—not just in the way bodies need each other, but in the way storms crave wind, in the way secrets beg to be whispered into skin. And that need was dangerous. That need could make me reckless. That need could cost me everything.

I closed my eyes and took a breath that burned my lungs. I had to start calming down. I had to draw the line before I crossed into something irreversible. He couldn't know how much he had me. That would give him too much power—and I'd lose the last bit of control I was clinging to.

What I needed was clarity, but clarity was a luxury lust didn't allow.

And as I dried my hands and stared again at that mask I'd have to wear, the truth settled like lead in my stomach: If I felt anything like this tomorrow at the office, I knew I was going to do something I'd regret. Something worth more than just a reprimand or a raised eyebrow.

Something fireable.

So what now?

That was the question that hung over me like the sword of Damocles. And I had the rest of the day—just today— to find the answer.

I stared into the mirror a moment longer, chewing on my bottom lip, trying to ignore the voice in my head that had now grown into a roar. "Maybe just once more…" It whispered like a devil draped in silk. "One more time, and that's it. You'll get it out of your system."

But that was a lie, wasn't it? I knew it. Just like I knew that if I walked into his room again, if I let his hands explore me one more time, I'd be gone. My control would dissolve like sugar on the tip of his tongue. If I hadn't already, I'd fall, and the thought terrified me more than I wanted to admit.

I tried to steady myself with logic, with reason. Tried to convince myself that one more time could be a clean ending. Like a final scene in a steamy film. But logic didn't stand a chance against the heat pulsing between my legs or the memory of his breath against my skin. Every inch of me still ached from the night before—in the best way possible—and the ache didn't fade, it simmered, waiting to boil over.

"Wait for him," I told myself. "If it was meant to happen, let it be his move. Let it be natural. Let it unfold."

But the waiting? The waiting was a kind of torture.

The fire between my legs was screaming, clawing, demanding. It was no longer a whisper, but a primal cry. My body betrayed me whenever I tried to pull away from the thought. I clenched my thighs in frustration, as if that could somehow contain the need that throbbed like a heartbeat—urgent, wild, alive.

And the more I told myself "no," the more vividly I imagined "yes."

It was like trying not to think of an elephant, and suddenly I was deep in a jungle of that thought—hot, sweaty, rugged, relentless. And yes—yearning. God, yearning.

I gripped the sink edge and closed my eyes.

"Jeez," I muttered under my breath, "get a hold of yourself."

But how? When your own body has become your enemy? When every inhale carried his scent from memory, every flash of heat behind your eyelids played scenes like a private reel you couldn't turn off?

I straightened, smoothed my dress, and fixed my hair. Professional. Composed.

But underneath?

I was a ticking bomb laced in silk and secrets.

And the only thing that could diffuse me… was the very thing I was trying to escape.

I left the washroom with a plan—to breathe, to regroup, to shut the box and padlock it with professionalism. But the moment I stepped back into the seminar room, the walls started closing in again. My colleague, one of the few who paid attention to the nuance of my presence, tilted her head and gave me a look that cracked the veneer I'd tried so hard to reapply.

"You okay? You don't seem yourself," she said softly.

Not myself? If only she knew how deeply true those words were. I nodded vaguely, muttered something about needing air, and slipped out before I said too much.

I was halfway down the corridor when fate decided to mock me—and there he was. Tall. Calm. That familiar presence that made everything in me jolt. My heart kicked up like a racehorse at the gate, and my knees threatened mutiny.

"Hey," he said, his voice too warm, too casual. But there was something beneath it—curious, alert. "You alright?"

I could've laughed. Was I alright? I was unravelling thread by thread, and he had no idea he was the needle pulling it all loose.

"I'm not feeling myself," I replied, and for once, my mouth honoured my brain. It wasn't a lie. It wasn't the whole truth either—but when you're dangling on the edge of desire and disaster, even partial honesty feels like an act of valour.

He tilted his head. "Do you want to lie down?"

And there it was—the invitation disguised as concern. An opening I had both dreamed of and dreaded since Friday. But something in me—something I didn't know I still had—rose and took the wheel.

"No," I said gently, firmly. "I just need some air. I'll be fine."

He smirked. A slow, knowing curve of the lips that made my stomach knot.

"With the way you look right now, you'd be lucky to make it to the exit door without collapsing."

I rolled my eyes, but I could feel the heat in my cheeks. He stepped closer, and instinctively, I leaned into him as he reached for my arm, steadying me like porcelain. His touch was light and effortless, but it lit a fire inside me that had only been smouldering seconds ago—now it was blazing.

I shouldn't have needed his help. I shouldn't have wanted his closeness.

But there I was—shoulder to chest, inhaling his scent, letting his hand wrap around mine like it had every right to.

The stronger I wanted to be, the weaker I became. And now, with him right next to me, breathing the same air, I realized something terrifying.

I wasn't just resisting him anymore.

I was resisting myself.

The moment the elevator dinged, I snapped out of my haze and realized I had walked in the opposite direction of fresh air. Unconsciously, I hadn't been seeking air—I had been walking straight into the fire.

His room was quiet, dimly lit, and cooler than I remembered. Maybe it was just me who was burning up. He guided me gently to the bed, his palm steady at my back like a compass I had stopped questioning. I sat, and he pressed a bottle of water into my hand like I was a fragile thing, something precious and breakable. That tenderness should've soothed me, but it only fanned the ache.

He tucked a loose strand of hair behind my ear and kissed my forehead—soft, lingering, reverent. Like I was holy.

"I'll head back down," he said, his voice gentle. "But if you need anything—anything at all—call me. No hesitation."

I nodded, but didn't trust myself to speak. He walked to the door and left with that careful kind of restraint that only made me feel more unsteady.

The door closed behind him.

One second.

Two.

Three.

By the fourth, I was calling.

My voice was barely above a whisper, but the words were fierce. "Come back. Now."

I stood, or tried to. My knees buckled slightly, and I caught myself on the edge of the bed. Just in time, the door swung open. He was there again—breathless, concerned, ready. His hands reached for me, steadying me like I mattered more than anything else in the world.

And in that moment, everything clicked.

The no had been weakening me. The restraint, the distance, the denial—I had worn them like armour, but they had started to crack the moment he touched me at the elevator. Saying yes wasn't surrender.

It was power.

Because the second I let go, I came back to life.

I stood up straight. My body wasn't trembling anymore. My eyes locked onto his like I finally saw clearly. He looked at me like he was still unsure of what I needed.

But I wasn't.

"I don't want to talk," I whispered, stepping into him. "I don't want to think. Just… make me forget the rules."

He hovered, uncertain, his brows creased with genuine concern. "Maybe you should lie down," he said softly, like he was afraid I'd break if he touched me too hard, or vanish if he blinked too fast. "I can come back once you've—"

"No," I cut in, my voice firm, clear, unwavering. "I've never felt stronger."

And I meant it.

Because something had shifted. That slow unravelling I'd felt earlier in the day—the heat, the confusion, the ache for control—had settled into something solid, something real. Saying yes wasn't a moment of weakness. It was the moment I returned to myself. Fully. Fiercely.

He studied me for a second, searching my face, maybe looking for hesitation. But I held his gaze with all the weight of the woman I was in that moment. Not lost. Not unsure. Just… lit up from within.

And when I stepped into him, hands firm against his chest, mouth just inches from his—he felt it. The change. The hunger.

He backed up just slightly, breath caught, as if something ancient had woken in him. Not fear—no, not that. It was reverence. That primal flash in his eyes told me everything: he saw me. Not just the woman he'd touched before, but the fire behind the woman. And it called to something wild in him.

The tension snapped.

His hands gripped my waist, tight, pulling me into him with a sudden urgency. There was no more hesitation. My lips met his in a kiss that didn't ask for permission—only submission to the inevitable. My strength made him bold. His boldness made me wild.

I pushed his jacket off his shoulders, and he let it fall to the floor without care. His fingers slid beneath my dress like they belonged there—like they had always belonged there—and I tilted my head back as his mouth found my neck again, softer this time, like he was tasting what he had already claimed.

He laid me back on the bed, but I pulled him with me—this wasn't something I'd be passive in. No, I was leading him now, and the way he followed told me everything. He wasn't afraid anymore.

He was hungry.

And I was about to feed every part of him.

His kisses were like sweet nectar—liquid fire wrapped in velvet, poured over skin too starved to resist. Each press of his lips wrote sonnets in heat, scrawled across my body like verses meant only for me. There was no room for thought anymore. The office, the risks, the whisper of reason that used to echo inside my head—they were drowned beneath the roar of pulse and desire. My skin hummed. My breath came in stutters. My body? Singing. Loud and unapologetic.

I was undone. Unhinged in the most glorious, reckless way.

And he—God—he met me there. Matched me, inch for inch, breath for breath, as though this was the version of me he'd been waiting for. The one who didn't hold back. The one who didn't flinch under the weight of needing, or hide her hunger behind practiced restraint.

He wanted all of me, and he took it—not with force, but with finesse.

With precision that felt damn near supernatural.

I hated it.

Not him. Not the pleasure.

I hated how easily he read me. Like my body was a story he'd already memorized, underlined, highlighted. He knew every page before I even cracked open the cover. His hands skimmed over me like he was touching the familiar—mapping curves and hollows with a reverence that made my chest ache.

Every place he touched lit up under his hands like it had been waiting—hibernating—for him.

He'd press, stroke, bite, pause… and something would unravel in me. Places I hadn't known could feel like that suddenly pulsed under his mouth like they belonged to him.

And that terrified me.

Because surrendering your body is one thing.

But letting someone know it—own it, even in fleeting moments—that's something else entirely.

His grunts started slow.

Low and guttural, tucked in the back of his throat like he didn't mean to let them escape. But when they did… oh, God, when they did… it was gasoline on an already blazing fire.

Each sound he made gave me permission—no, invitation—to go further. To arch harder. Pull him closer. Let the need twist and writhe inside me, shameless and primal.

And I did.

I clawed at his back, teeth grazing his shoulder as he thrust with the kind of rhythm that said, "I know what I'm doing to you." I bit back moans until I couldn't. Scratches, gasps, tangled limbs—we were everything you're not supposed to be in a professional setting. But there was nothing clinical about this.

He didn't just fuck me.

He worshipped me.

He broke me open and rearranged the pieces like he had the right.

And I let him.

Because it didn't feel like giving something away—it felt like finally claiming it.

He moved like he knew the crescendo was coming, but he wasn't going to let me fall alone. He held me through every tremor, every stuttering breath, every impossible wave until I shattered again—head thrown back, thighs shaking, soul slipping somewhere outside of time.

When it was over, I laughed.

Quiet, disbelieving, almost drunk on the afterglow.

A laugh born from somewhere raw and bright. Half awe, half what the hell just happened.

All of this…

From a simple compliment.

One offhand remark about my glow.

A harmless comment had triggered an avalanche.

And now here I was—naked, glowing, tangled in him, and somehow completely reborn.

Neither of us moved.

There was no need.

He was still inside me, one arm looped around my waist like a tether, his breath warm against my neck. I didn't want to rush. Didn't want to speak. Because nothing we could say would make more sense than the silence now curling around us like a second skin.

Sweaty. Breathless.

Holy.

Like whatever storm we'd just walked through had washed something clean.

And maybe that was the scariest part of all.

We just stayed there—entangled, warm, breathing the same air in the quiet hum that follows when bodies have spoken in a language words can't touch. My skin, still slick with our sweat, felt like it pulsed against his. Every inch where we touched was still vibrating, like the echoes of his mouth, his hands, his hips hadn't quite faded yet.

His heartbeat raced under my palm, quick and heavy, the last sign of the chaos we'd just weathered. It made me smile. That his body was still reacting to mine, even in the stillness.

There was something sacred about this moment. A lull, like the ocean pulling back after the wave. No pressure to speak. No promises looming in the air. Just the soft, grounding rhythm of his chest rising beneath my cheek and the delicious weight of his hand gliding in slow, lazy circles along the small of my back. Not to ignite. Not to tempt. But to remember. To savour. Like he was touching me now to memorize what we'd just done. As if every curve and freckle had become a sacred map.

My leg stayed thrown over his, one thigh still nestled against his heat. Our limbs fit together too well—like puzzle pieces that had waited for this moment to snap into place.

And even though my body was wrung out—drenched in release and dripping in the softness that follows the storm, there was still something sparking beneath the surface.

Not urgent, not hungry. Just that steady hum. A low thrum of ease. Of knowing.

There was no shame.

No awkward shuffle of limbs, no reaching for the blanket to hide.

Just the warm, weightless haze of having been completely undone by someone, and not needing to apologize for it.

I tilted my head, brushing my cheek across his chest as I looked up at him.

His eyes were half-lidded, thick lashes damp from sweat we hadn't had time to notice before. His lips were parted slightly, and there was something dazed in his expression—like he was still somewhere in the wreckage of what we'd just created.

He looked at me like I was both the fire and the water that doused it.

Like I'd wrecked him in the best possible way.

I laughed, soft and breathy, the sound trembling against his collarbone.

"What?" he murmured, voice gravel and silk.

"You," I whispered, hiding my smile in the curve of his shoulder. "Just… you."

He chuckled—low, hoarse, rich with that afterglow that sits somewhere between disbelief and satisfaction. His lips brushed the crown of my head, a kiss so gentle it barely registered and yet somehow hit deeper than the ones that had come before.

And right then, wrapped in him, all heat and heartbeat and skin, I felt the most dangerous kind of safe.

No guards. No masks.

Nothing held back.

Not my heart. Not my body.

Not even the fire that had almost swallowed us whole.

Because here, in the afterglow—the quiet, golden space between what had just happened and whatever the hell came next—I felt held. Not just physically, but something more… something bone-deep.

I knew it couldn't last forever.

Reality was out there—looming beyond the walls, waiting with questions and consequences. But here, now, with his hand on my back and my breath still tangled with his…

I let myself stay.

Still naked. Still glowing.

Still *his*.

Even if just for now.

Midnight Fire

After the seminar, I went home, heels in hand and skin still buzzing from the last encounter—not just with him, but with myself. There was something different in my steps, something softer, looser, as though my body had finally exhaled after years of holding its breath. I kicked the door shut behind me, tossed my bag onto the nearest chair, and walked straight to the kitchen, unbuttoning my blazer as I moved, one slow flick of the wrist at a time.

I poured myself a glass of red wine—something bold, dry, smooth, like the way I wanted the rest of my day to feel. The first sip slipped past my lips like velvet, warming me from the inside out, and I leaned back against the counter with a breathy laugh, shaking my head at myself.

What was happening to me?

I was no longer the same woman who had come home from work two days ago—poised, polished, the picture of professionalism. That woman had gone through something intimate and electric, something that cracked her open and poured in this unfamiliar heat, this softness, this... glow. And now? She was giggling in her kitchen with bare feet, messy hair, and a wine glass she hadn't even meant to pour, remembering hands that had studied her like scripture.

It was still late afternoon, a golden kind of light spilling through the windows—warm and inviting—and I figured I'd earned a nap. Just a short one. A reward for being good. A way to escape the tension humming underneath my skin.

I undressed slowly, peeling off the layers of my workday like old stories I no longer needed to wear. Each garment slid down with a sigh—fabric whispering across my skin—until I was bare, wrapped in nothing but a robe and that lingering scent of him that still clung to me like a secret. I slipped under the sheets, still warm from the sun, and let myself melt into the silence.

But it wasn't a nap. It was a surrender.

I passed out so deeply I wasn't sure I'd dreamt at all—only floated in some space where the line between memory and fantasy no longer mattered. I woke up hours later, and everything felt deliciously heavy, like the world had slowed just for me. My limbs stretched languidly across the bed, one at a time, like a cat basking in the remnants of pleasure. Even the stretch felt indulgent—each muscle unfolding, every joint releasing, my spine arching with a little gasp of satisfaction.

The sheets were tangled around my legs like a lover refusing to let go, and I let myself stay there for a moment longer, warm and dazed, my body humming with quiet contentment. I touched my fingers lightly to my skin—not out of lust but reverence—marvelling at how alive I felt.

Refreshed. Relaxed.

Ruined in the most beautiful way.

And that low simmer was still there somewhere in my belly—waiting.

Tidying up felt like dancing. Not the kind done for show, but the kind where your soul leads and your body follows—carefree, unchoreographed, and perfectly in sync with the rhythm only you can hear. There wasn't any actual music playing, but in my mind, something soulful was on repeat. A beat pulsing with lightness, freedom, and the afterglow of something unforgettable.

I folded the throw on the couch as if it were silk. Fluffed pillows like they were clouds. Even the dishes clinking in the sink felt like percussion in the background of my mood. I was moving through the home like it was mine again, and more than that, I was mine again.

There was a bounce in my step that hadn't been there before. A tilt to my smile. I had never felt this light, this... alive.

And the strange thing was, it wasn't just because of Damien.

I'd spent the last few days in a whirlwind—of hunger, of heat, of surrender—and now, standing barefoot in my own space with the windows open and the world quiet, I finally felt the calm after the storm. Not broken. Not confused. Just... centred.

I thought about Damien and laughed—not the nervous, unsure kind of laugh I'd been managing at the seminar, but a real one. A full-bodied, belly-deep laugh that came from a place of peace. Yes, he had touched me in ways no one ever had. Yes, he'd made me feel things that had me unravelling in elevators and drifting in hallways. But now? Now I could look at it all with a clarity that felt earned.

I understood something now: there was a difference between what Damien did to me and what he did to my body.

The craving, the heat, the fire—it was real. My body had screamed, begged, whispered for him. But my soul? My soul had watched, waited, and learned.

And what I had learned was this: I could want him without losing myself. I could give in to desire and still be grounded.

Because now, I wasn't chasing something. I wasn't aching from emptiness. I had already tasted the storm and survived it—beautifully.

Back in control.

Back to myself.

And more alive than ever.

I moved through my space like a woman who had danced with fire and didn't burn. A woman who had said yes, then no, then yes again—not out of confusion but choice. A woman who could laugh at her own dramatic thoughts from earlier—elephants and all—and still feel sexy doing it.

I wiped down the last counter, dimmed the lights, and stood silently for a moment. Just breathing. Just being.

Whatever came next, I was ready.

As if on cue—no, seriously, like the universe had written it into the script—I sank into the couch, legs folded beneath me, freshly showered and with the last of the weekend tasks crossed off my mental list. Hair damp, skin still warm from the water, wine glass now half-full instead of half-empty. The mood was mellow. Soft. Like the exhale after a storm.

I'd declared my weekend officially over. I was done. No more drama, no more overthinking, no more temptation. I even smiled at the thought—like I'd outwitted some wild beast and reclaimed my peace.

Then my phone buzzed.

"Hey, what are you up to?"

Simple. Harmless. Casual.

Except it was Damien.

And suddenly, I was no longer on that couch—I was sixteen, heart fluttering like I'd just opened a note in class that read, "Do you like me? Yes or no." I fidgeted. Laughed at myself. I took a slow sip of wine as if trying to calm a fire that was barely simmering now.

Only this time… he didn't unravel me.

He didn't trigger some chaotic spiral. He didn't spark that same aching need. At least not immediately.

I typed back, carefully breezy:

"Nothing much, just finished chores and getting ready for another workweek. What about you?"

He replied fast. Too fast.

"Just finished a drink and sitting here in my room watching a movie. Wanna join me?"

Just. Like. That.

Seven words, and I was spinning again.

That was a chill, friendly offer to anyone else on this planet. But to me? It was an encrypted message in a language I wasn't fluent in.

Was he being sincere?

Was this platonic?

Was he bored?

Did he want something?

Was he… teasing?

My thoughts raced, each one interrupting the other like impatient kids in a classroom.

Say no—he'll understand.

Say yes—and you're inviting something.

Say maybe—and you'll seem indecisive.

Say nothing—and you're being dramatic.

God, why was this so hard? Why did he make everything feel so intense without even trying?

Time ticked.

My fingers hovered over my phone like it was a detonator. And then, that voice in my head—the one I'd been listening to lately, the calm one, the clear one—reminded me: You're in control now. You choose. You set the terms.

So I breathed. Composed myself. Re-centred.

I didn't feel that feverish heat that had once overtaken me. The fire wasn't roaring—it was embers now, manageable, warm rather than wild.

So I texted him:

"I'd like to join you if you're serious. I'm getting bored out of my mind at home."

True. Every word.

Then I added:

"Give me about an hour and I'll be there."

I put the phone down and took a deep breath. Not nervously—calmly.

This time, I wasn't walking into the lion's den.

I was walking into my story, on my terms.

Now… what to wear that says:

"I'm chill. I'm in control. But yes, I'm still hot as hell."

Still composed. Still confident.

But this time, it wasn't forced.

It wasn't some internal pep talk trying to mask a storm underneath—it was real. Rooted. Balanced.

I looked at myself in the mirror one last time before grabbing my bag. My eyes had a calm radiance, as if I had journeyed through a storm and emerged with a quiet kind of power. The kind that didn't need to announce itself.

What surprised me most was that the thought of Damien didn't send sparks running through me like a live wire anymore.

Instead, it made me… smile.

Soft. Grateful. A little amused.

I had stopped seeing him as a wildfire I couldn't control, and started seeing him as part of a moment—a beautiful, unexpected moment—that had simply passed through. Two ships, gently brushing in the night, lit up by moonlight, maybe even sharing cargo briefly… but still meant to sail in different directions.

I didn't want more from him.

And for the first time, I wasn't pretending when I said that.

So with my head held high and my lips curved into a knowing smile, I walked into the hotel like I had walked into a new chapter. Each step was deliberate, relaxed, but strong. I could feel the confidence pulsing through me—not loud or dramatic, but smooth and easy like a favourite rhythm playing just beneath my skin.

The lobby lighting caught the soft gleam on my skin, and the elevator mirrors reflected a woman who was not chasing anything anymore. I wasn't here because I couldn't stay away. I was here because I had chosen to come. I had chosen myself first—and Damien, whatever he was or wasn't, was no longer holding the strings.

When I reached his door, I wasn't anxious.

There were no butterflies, no war inside me.

Just presence. Just peace.

I knew, in that moment, whatever happened next—whether it was a movie and a glass of wine or quiet conversation until I left again—I would still walk away feeling whole.

I knocked once.

Silence.

Twice—louder this time.

Still nothing.

A part of me flared with irritation, thinking maybe this was one of Damien's games again. Perhaps he was teasing me, knowing full well what effect his silence would have.

But then, through the muted hum of the hallway, his deep voice slid through the door like silk against bare skin.

"Come in."

Two words.

That's all it took.

Everything I thought I had recovered—my control, my calm, the neat little box I'd shoved my emotions into—disappeared like a puff of smoke.

I opened the door and stepped into something that didn't feel like his hotel room anymore.

The lights were off.

Only candles lit the space—soft golden flames dancing gently like they were swaying to some rhythm I couldn't hear but definitely felt.

And the scent…

Warm, woody, a hint of spice.

It wrapped around me like a slow-burning fog, seductive and welcoming, blurring the lines between this world and something more primal.

I couldn't see him at first, but I kept walking in—cautiously, my voice unsteady, calling his name.

Part nerves.

Part curiosity.

Part a feverish, growing hunger I hadn't come here to feed—but now couldn't ignore.

Then, he emerged.

Standing there, tall and still, like a statue carved out of shadow and flame.

The flicker of the candlelight caught the glint of sweat on his skin, casting golden streaks across every contour of his chest, arms, and the lines of his abdomen—all of it unapologetically on display.

And he wasn't moving.

He was watching.

Letting me take him in, letting my eyes roam, allowing the air thicken with the weight of what this was.

He didn't need to say a word.

His body was speaking for him.

Every muscle, every inhale, every inch of him told me what he wanted—and this time, it wasn't just desire tangled up in chaos.

It was an invitation.

It was clarity.

It was him wanting me. Not needing me, not reacting to a moment, not swept away by confusion.

He wanted me.

All of me.

And it wrecked me.

I had wanted him before. In flashes, in fantasies. In those quiet moments when desire stirred beneath the surface like a secret.

But this wasn't a flicker.

This was a blaze.

And what undid me wasn't just my wanting—it was his. Raw. Honest. Unhidden.

He didn't hold it back. Didn't play coy or pretend he wasn't standing there, needing me just as much, maybe more.

It hit me like a wave. And everything I thought I needed to protect?

Gone. Melted.

There was no space left for fear.

Only heat.

Only him.

He stood like a commandment in the middle of the room —silent, still, and entirely at my mercy.

I could see it in the rise and fall of his chest, sharp and unsteady, like he was trying to hold himself together.

Trying and failing.

"Don't move," I said softly. It wasn't a request.

His jaw twitched, but he nodded once.

And then I started to undress.

Slowly. Deliberately.

One button at a time, the fabric sliding off my shoulders like a promise whispered against skin. His eyes followed every motion, but his body—he kept still. Just barely.

I removed my top and let it fall between us like a promise waiting to be claimed.

His breath hitched.

I didn't stop.

I turned slightly as I reached for the clasp of my bra, giving him only a glimpse of curve, of skin—teasing. My back arched, and I could almost hear the restraint groaning in his bones. When the straps fell down my arms, I didn't rush. I held his gaze the entire time.

Each piece I shed felt like shedding more than just clothes.

It felt like shedding caution. Control.

Or maybe—claiming it.

The way he watched me... he made me feel like every inch of exposed skin was a confession he'd been waiting to hear.

I stepped out of my pants with a bit of extra sway in my hips, toes brushing the discarded fabric as if this entire performance was second nature.

But it wasn't.

I just wanted him to believe it was.

Because the way he looked at me—like I was holy and forbidden all at once—made me bold.

Made me dangerous.

Made me everything I'd never let myself be.

When I finally stood bare before him, I took a beat. Let him look. Let him ache.

Then I moved closer.

Every step was a pull on the tension stretched between us.

His fists clenched at his sides. His eyes burned.

But he didn't touch me. Didn't move.

He just waited.

And when I reached him—when I finally pressed my body into his—skin to skin, heat to heat—He let out a sound so low, so guttural, it went straight to my core.

He was fire under my fingertips.

And I hadn't even started yet.

We had talked about watching a movie.

Something casual, forgettable—background noise to pretend the air between us wasn't crackling.

But the second his eyes lingered a moment too long… the script changed.

We weren't watching anything.

We were the movie.

Every breath, every brush of skin, every hungry pause— it all played like a slow-burn indie flick, raw and unscripted.

And I was the one directing it.

He was the frame.

The screen.

The soundtrack.

And right now, he was mine.

I ran my fingers down the line of his chest, and he arched —barely, beautifully—like tension pulled taut over a drum.

He was solid under my touch, carved like temptation in stone.

And that heat between us?

It wasn't just lust.

It was pressure—like something seismic was about to give.

I let my hand drift lower, grazing him, and felt the full weight of the moment throb beneath my palm.

Oh, now I understood why they called it wood.

Not just the hardness—but the strength. The weight. The grounding.

His body trembled.

Not from nerves.

From restraint.

And there was nothing more delicious than watching him unravel one shiver at a time.

I paused—just long enough for him to suck in a breath, sharp and audible.

Then, with a smile that bordered on wicked, I reached for his hand.

His palm met mine without hesitation.

There was something so trusting in that grasp.

Like even now, in the shift of power, he was still all in.

Willing. Waiting.

I led him to the bed—not dragging, not rushing, but with the kind of grace you use when moving sacred things.

Each step padded with intention.

Each glance a command.

When I kissed him, it wasn't about hunger.

It was about possession.

A slow, deep claiming.

Our mouths moved like we were syncing breath, syncing heartbeats—and as I backed him onto the mattress, he followed without a word.

He lay there, chest rising, waiting.

Watching.

His pupils blown wide like he couldn't tell if he was being worshipped or devoured.

Maybe both.

Because this wasn't the same man who had once taken me apart with his hands and his mouth.

This was a different Damien.

One who had handed me the reins, opened himself wide to be known. To be guided.

And the power of it—the heady, velvet-slick ache of being the one in control—nearly undid me.

Guiding his hands.

Dictating the pace.

Choosing what got touched and what got teased.

It was intoxicating.

Not just the dominance—but the devotion.

He wasn't just lying there.

He was offering himself.

And that lit something feral inside me.

A hunger not just to take, but to teach. To show him what it meant to be truly wanted.

Because this wasn't about sex anymore.

This was about worship.

About trust strung tight like a violin string.

About letting someone in—not just on you, but under your skin.

And God, I wasn't done.

Not even close.

As I got on top of him and slowly swallowed him whole, inch by inch while savouring every bit of the motion, his grunt came low and brutal—ripped from somewhere deep in his chest, dragged out like I'd punched the air from his lungs. It wasn't delicate. It wasn't sweet. It was savage.

And it detonated something inside me.

The sound lit me up like a match struck in the dark—violent and sudden, flames licking the insides of my thighs, pulsing behind my eyes, setting off fireworks that had no rhythm, no mercy. I clenched around the echo of it, started grinding and grinding harder, chasing that broken music he was making like a woman possessed.

Because it wasn't just noise—it was surrender.

A raw, guttural admission that he'd come completely undone beneath me. That I had done this. Bent him. Broke him. Turned his control into rubble.

And God, I wanted more.

I needed to make him sing that sound again. Wanted to carve it into my spine, let it echo inside me every time I closed my eyes. My hips moved with no grace now—just greed. A pounding, primal rhythm that made the bed moan beneath us, that made his grip on the sheets white-knuckled and shaking.

He was trying to hold on.

I wasn't letting him.

I dragged my nails down his ribs—hard enough to make him gasp—and clamped my mouth to the curve of his neck, biting down until I felt the heat of his pulse throb under my tongue. He bucked under me, wild and wordless, and it only made me grind harder, ride faster, drive him deeper into the mattress like I wanted to leave him there permanently marked.

Every thrust was a demand.

Every gasp, an answer.

His hands—helpless, frantic—finally found my hips, fingers digging in, bruising with intention. Not guiding. Not leading. Just holding on as I pushed him over that edge again, and again, and again.

It wasn't fucking anymore.

It was war.

It was worship.

It was need so sharp it cut.

I pressed my forehead to his, breath slick and shallow between us, and let myself fall all the way into it. Into him.

Still moving. Still claiming.

And I wasn't slowing down.

Not until he broke completely.

Not until I took everything.

That groan—it wasn't just sound anymore. It was the collapse of his composure, torn loose from somewhere deep and ragged. It was pure desperation, echoing through his chest like a war drum. And I fed on it.

I didn't ease up. I pushed.

I rode the edge of him like a storm surge—grinding slow and deep with a control so tight it bordered on cruelty. My fingers released his wrists only to slide down his chest, nails dragging just hard enough to leave red trails in their wake. He shivered, hips twitching beneath me, eyes wild and pleading. But I didn't stop to soothe. I wasn't here to be gentle.

I was here to ruin him.

I got up not to stop, but to take over him in every way I knew how. I wasn't ready to crash the dam just yet. I licked a bead of sweat from his collarbone, nipped the soft skin just above his heart, then dragged my tongue lower, lower, lower—watching him tremble under every inch of denied pleasure. I didn't need to look up to know his eyes were on me, desperate and drowning. I could feel it in the way he pulsed under my touch. He was unravelling—beautifully, helplessly—each second another thread yanked loose.

When I finally took him into my mouth, I didn't tease.

I devoured.

And when he arched up, crying out from the shock of it, I slammed my hand flat against his hip, pinning him down. "Stay."

He obeyed. God, he obeyed. His knuckles went pale as he fisted the sheets, his breath shattered in my ears like glass. He was panting now—fighting to keep still, fighting me, fighting himself—and losing. I felt the quake begin again, the tremor in his thighs, the low, almost tortured growl spilling from his lips like he couldn't contain the storm I'd made of him.

I didn't stop.

Couldn't.

Because I wasn't chasing an orgasm.

I was chasing submission.

And when his whole body seized under my mouth, when his voice broke into something raw and strangled and mine, I knew—

This wasn't just power anymore.

It was possession.

And I wasn't giving it back.

I didn't just want him—I wanted to break him open and drink the want out of him. I wanted to press into the softest parts of him and pull out the deepest sounds, the rawest reactions, the ones he'd never made for anyone else.

I slid down, slow like syrup, keeping my eyes on him the entire way. He was watching me with that look— desperate, wrecked, reverent. The look of a man who had surrendered every ounce of control and knows he'll never be the same again.

I took him in hand again, teasing with the lightest touch, just enough to make his thighs twitch and his breath stutter. I licked the tip, just once, a slow circle, and the groan that escaped his mouth hit me straight in the core. I felt it between my legs before it even hit my ears. He was unravelling beneath me, and I hadn't even started.

I took him deeper, slow, deliberate, giving him just enough to feel what he could have, then pulling back. My hand wrapped around the base, stroking in rhythm with my mouth—wet, warm, and merciless in its pace. His fingers fisted in the sheets. His hips twitched. He tried to hold still, but his body was begging to move.

"Please..." he rasped. The word cracked in the air, desperate and unfinished.

I moaned in response, the vibration making him shudder. Then I looked up at him—his eyes were wild now, wide with disbelief, like he couldn't believe this was real, like he couldn't believe what I was doing to him. That I had reduced him to this.

And I wasn't done.

I stood, slow and deliberate, wiping my mouth with the back of my hand like I'd just feasted—and in a way, I had. He reached for me again, but I climbed on top, straddling him, holding his wrists down again, smiling as I rocked gently against him, not letting him in yet, just grinding, teasing, wet and warm right over the spot he wanted to be buried in.

"You're not going to last," I whispered with a smirk.

"Try me," he growled back.

So I did.

And when I finally sank on him, slow, inch by glorious inch, I didn't just take him—I claimed him.

His whole body arched beneath me, guttural moans filling the room.

The way he filled me had my entire body pulsing—tight, wet, alive. I stayed there for a moment, still and locked in place, just letting the fullness stretch and throb between us. His chest heaved under me, hands still pinned, but his hips were already betraying him, desperate to meet mine, to thrust up and take back even a sliver of control.

But I wasn't ready to give it.

I began to move—slow, deliberate, rolling my hips in tight circles, grinding down so every flicker of friction landed right where it made me see stars. He cursed low and long, the kind of sound that made my walls clench around him. I felt the pressure building like a tide about to surge every second I rode him.

My name escaped his mouth in a broken moan—drawn out, needy, sacred.

His wrists struggled under my grip, his body arching to meet mine, but I leaned down, licked the sweat from his collarbone, and whispered, "Stay."

He did.

But barely.

I changed the rhythm—slamming down hard, then pulling up slow, teasing, repeating, using my whole body to torture him sweetly. His muscles trembled under me. His breath came in bursts. I could see him unravelling again, could feel how close he was, how tightly his body was coiled, how much he wanted to come but wouldn't dare until I let him.

"Tell me," I breathed, my lips brushing his ear, "what do you need?"

"You," he groaned, voice strangled. "Harder. Please. I need—"

I slammed down again, stealing his words, replacing them with a grunt so deep it rattled through my chest.

Then I let go of his wrists.

He flipped us without hesitation, landing above me with an urgency that made my whole body throb. I gasped, legs already locking around his waist, nails digging into his back as he started thrusting—slow, hard, deep.

He was claiming me now, but only because I had let him.

And that made every thrust feel like fire and thunder.

The sound of skin against skin filled the room, wet and wild, matched only by the music of our breathless cries. We weren't fucking anymore—we were chaos in motion. Pure hunger. Pure rhythm. Two bodies colliding at the edge of pleasure so sharp it bordered on pain.

And when I looked into his eyes—dark, blown, desperate—I knew…

I saw something wild in his eyes—something primal, reverent, almost afraid of how much he needed me. That desire turned me molten. I reached up, tugged his lip between my teeth, and whispered with a breathless laugh, "Don't hold back now."

And he didn't.

He drove into me with a force that knocked the breath out of my lungs, hips slamming into mine like thunder meeting earth. My legs wrapped tighter around him, anchoring him to me like I could fuse us together if I just held on hard enough.

His name spilled from my lips repeatedly, a chant, a confession, a warning.

The bed creaked in protest, sheets tangled beneath us like we were rewriting gravity. His hands roamed my body like he'd never seen it before, like every curve, every inch was something holy—something meant to be worshipped and devoured all at once. He pressed his forehead to mine, our sweat mixing, eyes locked as if we could see the moment coming before it hit.

"Look at me," he growled, voice low and deep.

I did.

I watched him come undone—his mouth parted, his body rigid, then shuddering as he let go deep inside me. And that, that—the raw, unfiltered way he surrendered —was what tipped me over the edge, too.

I came hard, back arching, body clenching around him, and everything else dissolved. The world went white behind my eyelids. All I could hear was the chorus of our moans. All I could feel was the firestorm between us crashing and crashing again until there was nothing left but trembling limbs and shallow gasps.

He collapsed beside me, pulling me into him like I was the answer to a question he'd spent his whole life asking.

And for a long, slow moment… we just breathed.

We laid there, a tangled mess of limbs and sheets, wrapped around each other like vines too entwined to separate. The only sounds were our breaths—slow, uneven, but gradually syncing, like our hearts were learning to speak in the same rhythm.

His chest rose and fell beneath my cheek, warm and solid, like a grounding force after a storm. I traced small circles on his skin with my fingertip, mind half-dazed, body still humming with aftershocks. There was no rush now. No need to speak. We had said everything in the way we moved, in the way we touched, in the way we surrendered.

He kissed the top of my head, not with urgency but with something softer—something tender and real. I felt his fingers graze along my spine, lazy and reverent, as if he was still exploring but with no destination in mind. Just pleasure in presence.

We were still glowing—still radiating heat, but not the searing kind. This was the afterburn. That slow, golden warmth that seeps into your bones and makes you want to stay right there forever.

The candles still flickered in the corners of the room, shadows dancing across the walls. Time had paused for us, or maybe it had melted entirely. I had no idea what hour it was. I didn't care.

He whispered something—I didn't even catch the words—but it made me smile. Whatever it was, it was laced in affection, maybe awe, maybe disbelief. I kissed his jaw, his neck, then tucked myself into him again, breathing him in, memorizing the weight of this exact moment.

My body felt like silk and flame all at once, and my mind? For the first time in forever… it was quiet.

I didn't know what would come next. But right then, tangled up in him, in this hush of shared euphoria—I didn't need to know.

His breath was steady now, slower, deeper—almost like waves lapping against the shore. I let my eyes flutter closed, listening to the rise and fall of his chest beneath me, that soft rhythm becoming my lullaby. My fingers were still loosely intertwined with his, neither of us willing to let go, even in rest.

He shifted slightly, not to move away, but just enough to pull me closer, as if sleep would only come if he felt every inch of me against him. And I didn't resist. I couldn't. I fit perfectly in that space—his arms around me, the warmth between us, the softness of the sheets cradling our bodies like a secret we didn't want the world to know yet.

His heartbeat was slow, almost drowsy, and I followed its rhythm into that sweet, slipping place between wakefulness and dreams. I felt him press one last kiss into my hair, not out of passion this time, but something more profound. A gentle surrender. A silent thank-you.

And then, in the hush of flickering candlelight and cooling skin, we drifted.

Two heartbeats.

One quiet night.

And a sleep so complete, so safe, it felt like a home we'd both forgotten we needed.

The Ultimate Dopamine Rush

We had certainly passed out sometime after midnight, our bodies finally surrendering after a storm of passion. Yet when I stirred just before dawn, I wasn't tired. I wasn't sore. I was glowing—from the inside out. A warmth still coursed through me like the embers of a fire that had blazed all night long and now glowed steady and low. The sheets were a tangled mess of stories, the room still scented with a blend of candle wax, his cologne, and the trace of our skin.

I blinked slowly, the world hazy in the faint lavender-blue glow of morning. His body, lying beside mine, was stretched out in a picture of tranquillity—bare, golden, and softly rising and falling with each breath. His face had softened in sleep, almost boyish, lips parted slightly as if he was still whispering my name in some dream I hoped I had starred in.

I should've gotten up. I had work, a life to get back to—but I couldn't bring myself to leave. Not yet. I let my fingers trail lightly along the ridge of his collarbone, the dip between his shoulder and chest where I had nuzzled into the night before. My leg, draped over his, clung just a little tighter, my skin greedy for that quiet heat. I told myself I didn't want to wake him—he looked too peaceful—but the truth was, I needed one more moment. One more taste of this serenity.

It wasn't just lust. It wasn't just chemistry. It was dopamine. A euphoric high I hadn't expected. The kind that came not from climax but from connection.

And as I laid there, my hand splayed across his chest, feeling the steady thump of his heart, I hoped—quietly, desperately—that he was dreaming about me. That maybe, in whatever world his mind had drifted to, he was still feeling my touch. Still hearing my voice. Still reliving what we'd created just hours before.

Part of me knew I had to let go. Get dressed. Face the day. But another part of me—perhaps the most genuine part—just wanted to stay like this, wrapped in the aftermath of a night that had melted boundaries and rewritten every rule of what I thought intimacy could be.

So I held him. And in that still, perfect silence before the world stirred, I let myself believe that moments like this were more than just fleeting. They were transformative. And I—glowing, tangled, and completely at peace—was transformed.

I was enjoying my body against his like a cat in a sunbeam—stretching into every inch of warmth he offered, pressing myself into the smooth, solid comfort of his skin. Every point of contact, from the soft curve of my thigh resting across his hip to my cheek nestled against his shoulder, felt like a secret I didn't want to share with the world outside. The silence wrapped around us like a second blanket, warm and unbroken except for the sound of his steady breath and the rhythmic beating of his heart beneath my palm.

I knew the moment was ending—the weekend, the spell, whatever bubble we had built between us—it had reached its final edge. And I dreaded that edge. The thought of letting go, of peeling myself away from him and returning to the real world, was almost unbearable. For a fleeting second, I actually thought about pulling him closer, whispering for him to call in sick, and slipping right back into the dream. Just one more hour. One more morning wrapped in this hazy bliss. But I let the idea float away, laughing softly at my fantasy. It was silly, romantic, maybe even selfish—but real life waited, and I needed to meet it with the same grace I'd shown myself this weekend.

Still, I didn't move.

My body didn't budge. My arms, draped across his chest, felt as if they were bound there by invisible silk threads, unwilling to release their grip. I was savouring him, taking mental photographs of how his skin felt warm and impossibly smooth under my fingertips. I rubbed slow, lazy circles on his chest, letting my fingers memorize the terrain. It wasn't possessive in the traditional sense, but there was a quiet claim in it—like I was marking my territory, not to own, but to remember.

This wasn't about not wanting to let him go. This was about not wanting to let this go—the feeling, the closeness, the freedom I'd found in him and in myself. The skin-to-skin contact felt sacred now, a final prayer before I slipped out of the temple we'd built in the hours and minutes before.

I didn't cry. I didn't pout. I just stayed a little longer. Letting my body speak for me. Letting the warmth between us echo what words could never fully say.

Somehow—God knows how—I found myself touching him again. It wasn't planned. It wasn't conscious. It was instinct. A pull as natural as breath, as reckless as lust. My fingers slid lower, grazing over the thick outline of him—already hard, already waiting. Like he'd been dreaming of me, like his body had felt me before his mind could wake.

He throbbed under my touch—alive and pulsing with heat. Tension coiled so tightly it vibrated beneath my palm. Rage, desire, desperation—it was all there, swelling against my fingers like a promise wrapped in threat. My breath hitched. I froze.

I should've left then. I meant to.

But my hand didn't.

It stayed.

It claimed.

I fondled his rigid heat, slow and firm, and he twitched like I'd shocked him awake. A low growl rumbled from deep in his throat—barely conscious, but fully animal. That sound struck me like lightning to the spine. He didn't speak, didn't open his eyes, but his hips shifted, rising into my hand, chasing the friction like a man starved for touch.

And me? I broke.

I leaned in, mouth at his ear, lips brushing skin still warm from dreams. "You're not getting rid of me that easily," I whispered.

He stirred again, this time with intention. His hand shot out, gripping my wrist tightly. Possessive. Still half-asleep, but his body knew exactly what was happening. And he didn't stop me. He guided me. He welcomed it.

I climbed over him, one leg at a time, bare thighs straddling his stomach, pressing down with the weight of everything I'd been holding back. My other hand braced on his chest—his skin hot, muscles tensed, heart hammering like a war drum.

His demanding flesh stood like a demand between us, slick at the tip and straining for me. I rocked against it slowly, letting it slide through the wet, quivering hunger between my thighs without letting him in. Teasing him. Teasing myself. My breath came hard and fast as I dragged my body over his, letting him feel every inch I had to offer.

Still not inside.

Still not enough.

His eyes finally opened—wild, unfocused, wrecked— and locked on mine. No words. Just that look. That look that said he was done pretending. Done holding back.

But I pressed my palm against his chest again, pinning him down with a slow smile.

"Not yet," I whispered.

And then I sank onto him.

Inch by slow, exquisite inch.

He choked on a moan, fingers digging into my thighs like he needed to anchor himself to keep from losing it. And maybe he did. Because I didn't just take him—I consumed him. I clenched around him, moved with purpose, dragged us both to the edge of something feral and final.

He met every thrust like it hurt not to. Like he'd been waiting for this moment his whole life and never thought he'd survive it.

And maybe neither of us would.

Because this wasn't goodbye.

This was obliteration.

And Monday?

Monday could wait.

He was inside me—hot, hard, twitching with need—and I hadn't moved much yet. Just enough to make him beg in every language his body knew. My hands pressed against his chest, feeling the stutter of his heartbeat under my palms, and then—

His voice broke through the quiet like a velvet flame, low and gravelly with the remnants of sleep:
 "I hope you're not planning to start something you don't intend to finish... it'd be cruel to leave me hanging."

I froze for half a second—because God, that voice. That voice could melt glaciers. Could set off alarms. Could make a woman forget every sane thing she was ever taught about restraint.

A smirk tugged at my lips, part mischief, part surrender. "Cruel?" I murmured, shifting my hips ever so slightly—just enough to make him hiss through his teeth. "I haven't even gotten mean yet."

His words hadn't just invited me—they had unlocked me. The gates inside me flew open. Every unspoken fantasy I'd bottled up all weekend—the dark ones, the tender ones, the ones too bold to name—rushed forward in a torrent of need. I was done holding back. And he knew it. He wanted it.

What made it worse—or better—was the way he looked at me. Like he knew. Like he relished the game. Like every move I made closer to the edge only pulled him deeper into the abyss with me, and he'd go willingly.

Each time I gave in—a rougher roll of my hips, a deeper grind, a filthier rhythm—his eyes darkened with that same intoxicating approval. It was like being worshipped and devoured at the same time. That kind of knowing, that permission... it didn't just encourage me —it fed me. Turned my hesitation into hunger. Shame into power.

I leaned down, lips grazing the shell of his ear, voice low and thick with heat.

 "Oh, I plan to finish," I whispered, licking the last word off his skin. "But not quickly."

His breath hitched. His grip on my hips tightened—firm, commanding, but still letting me lead. Barely. And that subtle shift in pressure? That was his answer. The roles had changed. I wasn't just on top—I was in charge. But he could flip the script at any moment, and we both knew it.

My body thrilled at the danger.

I started to ride him in earnest now, grinding hard and slow, holding his stare with every stroke. His jaw clenched. His hands twitched with restraint. And still, I dragged it out—pushed him higher, tighter, until he was trembling beneath me again. Until every muscle in his body was screaming for release.

But I wasn't finished.

Not by a long shot.

"You said it would be cruel to leave you hanging," I whispered again, rolling my hips with a devilish slowness. "But baby, I like cruel."

He growled—growled—and in one sudden motion, he sat up, hands on my back, mouth crashing into mine. His kiss was savage, teeth and tongue and heat, and when he pulled away, his voice was thunder wrapped in velvet:

"Then finish me. Wreck me. I dare you."

And just like that, the fire I'd started?

He turned it into an inferno.

He flipped us and got on top. He moved inside me like he knew me—every gasp, every clench, every place I broke open just to be put back together by his hands, his mouth, his everything. I couldn't tell where he ended and I began. All I knew was that I wanted more. Needed more. And he gave it—merciless and tender, like worship turned into war.

He kissed the corner of my mouth, my jaw, my neck— each one a vow he made without speaking. My body arched for him, every nerve strung tight and singing. And when his teeth found that spot just beneath my collarbone, I shattered. Not all at once—but slowly, gloriously, like glass melting under flame.

"I've got you," he whispered, voice rough, reverent. "Let go."

And I did.

I let go of the world. Of the clock ticking. Of every piece of armour I'd ever worn to survive. Because in his arms, I wasn't surviving—I was living. I was craving. I was seen.

He held my face in both hands like I was something holy, something rare, and kissed me like he wanted to keep the taste of me locked in his lungs forever. And when his name broke from my lips—raw, gasped, half a prayer— he growled my name back with a fury that made my toes curl and my soul stretch wide open.

The rhythm grew desperate. Delirious. Like we were racing toward something ancient and infinite. His body drove into mine with a sacred kind of violence, the kind that left no part untouched, no part unloved.

Every cry, every breath, every tremble between us was a confession. A surrender. A promise.

He whispered my name like it was the only word he'd ever known—slow, husky, reverent. It wasn't a question. It wasn't even a need. It was a declaration, and it coiled around my spine like silk laced with fire. His grip on my hips tightened, anchoring me in place, not letting me run from what was coming—even if I'd wanted to.

But I didn't want to run. I wanted to drown.

Each thrust was deeper, more deliberate, more demanding. He wasn't chasing release—he was claiming territory. Drawing out every second like a musician drawing breath between the sweetest, most devastating notes. We were a heartbeat away from ruin, suspended in that beautiful, unbearable space where pleasure flirts with pain and surrender tastes like victory.

"God, you feel like sin," he growled against my throat. "Like you were made just to break me."

"You're already breaking," I breathed, dragging my nails down his back. "And I haven't even started."

A low, wicked sound rumbled from his chest—half laugh, half moan. "That mouth's gonna get you in trouble."

"I'm counting on it."

I could feel it building—thick in the air, thrumming under my skin, curling in my toes and pressing hot behind my eyes. He knew it too. I saw it in the way he looked at me. As if he were watching something sacred crack open. Like he wanted to see me break... but not yet. Not just yet.

"Don't," he breathed, forehead pressed to mine, voice laced with warning and need. "Not yet."

I whimpered, desperate, thighs trembling, but obeyed. Not because I had to—but because I wanted him to be the one to pull the final thread. I trusted him with that power. With all of it.

"I can't..." I whispered, voice ragged, "I'm right there."

His hand slid up my spine, grounding me. "You can. Stay with me."

"You're killing me..."

"No," he said, voice like gravel and smoke. "I'm remaking you."

Our bodies kept moving—slick, perfect friction, rhythm carved from instinct and reverence. His lips dragged across my throat, whispering things too sinful to survive the morning light.

"You're mine," he said, teeth grazing my collarbone.

"Always," I whispered. "I just need you to take me."

"I'm not taking you," he murmured, thrusting deep enough to steal my breath. "I'm keeping you."

And somehow, through the ache, the shaking, the impossible pressure climbing higher and higher inside me, I held on.

Because he hadn't told me to fall.

And I was waiting for that word, as if it were salvation.

Holding it in was punishment. Sweet, delicious punishment. I wanted to be strong, but it's nearly impossible when someone feels like they're tap-dancing on your walls. He handled me. He worshipped my body, and I never felt more wanted. Needed even. He gave me all my body needed. And in that moment, I shattered.

There was no holding back. No graceful descent. It hit like a storm surge—violent, breathtaking, total. My body convulsed around him as my scream tore from somewhere deep, somewhere wordless. But he didn't stop.

He kept going.

Relentless. Focused. Worshipful.

It was fireworks after fireworks—waves of pleasure that refused to let up, crashing over me until I couldn't tell where one ended and the next began. I wasn't even begging anymore—I was whimpering, sobbing, caught in the kind of euphoria that felt like it could crack open the sky.

And still, he didn't stop.

"Don't hold back," he growled into my ear, voice shaking with restraint. "Give it to me. All of it."

I couldn't answer. I was already gone. Already his. But that didn't stop him from taking more—pushing deeper, grinding harder, his breath hot against my skin like gasoline to a flame.

"Fuck—you're unreal," he groaned, briefly burying his face in my neck. "Look at me when you cum."

"I—I can't—"

"Yes, you can." His voice snapped like a command. "Look. At. Me."

And I did. I met his eyes through the haze—wide, wild, aching—and the second our gazes locked, something broke again inside me. My body clenched, legs trembling violently, and the scream that left me sounded more like a prayer than a cry.

He didn't falter. He didn't soften.

He drove into me as if this were the final performance of something sacred. As if he were leaving his name etched in my bones. Every touch, every thrust was a message.

Remember me.

His hands gripped my hips, guiding, anchoring, demanding. And I gave—more than I thought I had left —because the way he moved, the way he moaned, the way he looked at me like I was the only woman who'd ever mattered to him… it wrecked me.

"You feel like heaven," he murmured, voice hoarse, almost broken. "Like I was made for this. For you."

My fingers tangled in his hair, desperate, reverent. "Don't stop. Don't ever fucking stop."

"I won't," he panted. "Not until you know exactly what you are to me."

And God, he showed me.

Not just through thrusts, kisses, or the way he groaned my name over and over like it was the only word he'd kept sacred.

He showed me through the way he touched me. Attentive. Fierce. Intentional.

Like I wasn't just his partner in this storm—I was his gravity.

And I felt sexy. Not for any mirror, not for some rehearsed pose—but because of how he saw me. Like I was chaos and salvation. Like my pleasure was a map and he'd studied every contour until he could find his way blind.

And maybe that's what this was.

Not just lust. Not even love.

It was reverence.

And I didn't care if it was the end or the beginning. I only knew one thing:

He wasn't just inside me—he was written into me.

His hand slid beneath my thigh, lifting me, adjusting the angle like he was fine-tuning an instrument he knew by heart. The next thrust knocked the breath out of me. Deep. Deliberate. Devastating.

"You're not going yet," he rasped, breath hot against my jaw. "Not until I say."

My body jolted at his voice—commanding, reverent, cracked open with need.

"Please…" I breathed, voice wrecked, trembling on the edge of sobbing. "I need—God, I need—"

"I know what you need," he growled, each word like gravel against silk. "And I'm gonna give it to you. But you're gonna feel it. Every. Fucking. Second."

His hips moved with punishing precision, each roll of his body timed to wreck me just a little more. He wasn't chasing release—he was crafting it. Layer by layer. Sound by sound. Until I couldn't tell if I was begging or cursing or crying his name just to stay tethered to the moment.

"You think I'm gonna let you forget this?" he murmured, lips brushing my temple. "Nah, baby. You're gonna feel me every time you breathe."

I choked on a moan, nails digging deeper, clutching at him like he was the only thing holding me to earth.

"Say it," he demanded. "Tell me you're mine."

"I'm yours," I gasped, arching into him. "God—I'm yours, I'm fucking yours—"

"That's right," he said, nearly a snarl, but laced with something else—something tender beneath the dominance. "All of you. This—" his hand slid to my throat, not choking, just holding, "—this mouth, this body, this soul. Mine."

My whole body trembled. A sob bubbled up from deep in my chest, but it wasn't pain—it was surrender. The kind that breaks open, not down.

He kissed me then—hard and claiming, like a signature at the end of a contract neither of us had to read. And when his lips broke from mine, he stayed just a breath away.

"Cum for me," he whispered. "Fall apart in my hands."

And God help me... I did.

I was trembling—no, quaking—under him, around him, through him. My breath came in ragged bursts, not air but need, spilling from my lungs like something holy had been ripped from them. He was still inside me moving with that cruel, sacred patience—slow, profound, devastating. Every stroke was as if he were memorizing the shape of my soul from the inside out.

His body pressed into mine like gravity, like truth. He had me pinned in every way a person can be pinned—flesh, mind, spirit. There was no distance between us. No separation. I wasn't under him anymore—I was with him, of him. Unravelled and reborn in the same breath.

And he was still holding back.

His whole body thrummed with restraint, like he was gripping the edge of a cliff by his teeth just to give me these last few seconds suspended in the unbearable beauty of almost. His lips hovered above mine, not kissing, just breathing me in like I was the first clean inhale after drowning.

I whispered his name—fractured, fervent—and it shattered something in him.

He hissed through his teeth. "You feel that?" His voice was wrecked, trembling. "That's me—about to fucking lose it."

I nodded, whimpering, unable to form anything but yes. Please. Now.

His hand slid down my side, gripping my hip like he was claiming it—like it had always been his. "You want it?" he asked, not teasing—daring.

"I want everything," I gasped. "I want you to ruin me."

And then—

He snapped.

He drove into me with a force that lit the world on fire. The air ripped from my lungs as a scream tore from my chest—raw, involuntary, true. My body arched up, wrapped around him like I could possess him in return, like I could pull him deeper and keep him there forever.

He was speaking—half growls, half worship—his voice cracking against my skin as he moaned my name like a psalm, like a weapon, like a confession. And every word was etched into me like scripture.

"God, you feel like fucking heaven," he groaned. "You're mine. You hear me? You're fucking mine."

I shattered—no warning, no restraint—into a thousand pieces of pleasure. I came with a violence that felt like being set free from the inside, like my soul had been waiting for this exact devastation. But he didn't stop. He couldn't stop. He was chasing his ruin now, and I was the path to it.

"Don't let go," I begged, breathless and wrecked. "Please—don't let go—"

"I'm not," he growled. "I'm not going anywhere."

And then he fell with me.

His release slammed through him in a soundless roar, his whole body shaking against mine. He was inside the quake of it, buried in it, buried in me, coming like it had been building for lifetimes. I felt every twitch, every throb, every broken breath against my neck as he gave it all. Every piece. Every promise. Every ounce of control he had held so tightly until now.

The room disappeared.

We existed only in the aftermath—breathing each other in, bodies locked, souls still singing. It was more than climax. More than touch.

It was a reverberation.

And in that quiet, tangled, sacred silence, he looked down at me, eyes wild and soft all at once, and said with the voice of a man who had just found home in fire:

"You'll feel me for the rest of your life."

And I would.

God, I would.

The stillness that followed felt almost unreal, like the world outside our window had paused out of respect for what had just happened between us. The storm was over, but the air was still charged, humming with the weight of everything we'd said without words.

Our bodies remained tangled, too intertwined to tell where I ended and he began. His skin was warm beneath my cheek, his heartbeat a slow, steady rhythm I could've sworn had synced to mine. I traced it with my fingertips —lazy, looping patterns on his chest, like if I stopped touching him, I might forget this was real.

He shifted just slightly, enough to press a kiss to my hair. Nothing hungry. Nothing demanding. Just presence. Intention.

"Did I leave a mark?" he asked softly, almost teasing—but not quite. There was something raw behind the words, something honest. Maybe even a little scared.

I didn't open my eyes. Just smiled and whispered, "All over me."

He exhaled slowly, and I felt it ripple through his whole body, down to where our legs were still tangled beneath the covers. His thumb brushed over the back of my hand—slow, reverent, like he wasn't just touching skin, but something deeper. Something permanent.

We lay like that for a while, not measuring time, not needing to.

Eventually, I rolled just enough to face him, our noses barely touching, foreheads close enough to share breath. His eyes were half-lidded but locked on me, pupils dark and soft. I looked at him the way you look at something from which you're afraid to blink away.

"I don't want to fall asleep," I murmured, voice feather-light.

He smiled—crooked and sleepy and real. "Then don't," he said. "Just stay here."

Here.

In his arms. In the warmth still lingering in the sheets. In this fragile, golden hour where nothing from outside could reach us.

I nodded, resting my forehead against his and closing my eyes anyway.

We didn't speak again. There were no declarations. No promises. Just two bodies recovering from something holy, two souls wrapped so tightly around the silence, even the morning didn't dare interrupt.

And as the sun climbed higher, soft light spilling across our skin, I realized—I wasn't just lying beside him.

I was home.

I was high on dopamine, and it felt like the release wasn't stopping—waves still crashing long after the tide had pulled back. My brain was foggy, and my thighs trembled as if I would need to learn how to walk again. I had only heard a few women whisper about something they called "cloud nine," their eyes going distant with memory. And now I understood. It had clicked. It was real.

I had come harder than I ever had in my life—again and again, until I couldn't tell where one orgasm ended and another began. My body felt as though it had melted, spilled over, and reformed into something softer, sweeter, and wholly undone. The pleasure had lingered like a flavour, like sugar on the tongue, and I was floating in it. Floating in him.

After catching my breath, I kissed him—slow, deep, like a thank you and maybe a promise. My lips lingered on his just long enough to leave an echo. Then I whispered that I had to go home and get ready for work. I watched his eyes when I said it. Not I have to leave, not this is over, just a soft ushering in of reality, deliberately vague, gently true. I didn't want to close the door too firmly. I didn't want to admit what I hadn't fully named yet.

I hoped he understood what I couldn't quite say—that I was leaving, yes, but not all of me. That something of me was still in his bed, in his breath, in the warmth still pressed into those tangled sheets. That I hadn't fallen—not yet—but the descent had begun, and I wasn't bracing for the impact anymore.

The shower I took was quick, but nothing about it felt ordinary. My skin was still buzzing, almost bruised by bliss. My lips, swollen from the kind of kissing that felt like confession. My legs, still shaky beneath me like I'd been wrecked by a truth too exquisite to stand on.

And when I stepped back into my clothes—his scent still clinging to them like a secret—I knew something inside me had shifted. I wasn't just walking into a Monday morning. I was stepping into it as a woman rewritten. Bold. Claimed. Glowing from the inside out.

This weekend hadn't changed everything.

But it changed enough.

It reminded me of who I could be when I let myself feel. When I let myself want. When I let someone in far enough to touch the parts of me I'd tucked away.

It reminded me of what it was like to be fully seen. Completely taken. Gloriously, recklessly, wanted.

THE END

www.ingramcontent.com/pod-product-compliance
Lightning Source LLC
Chambersburg PA
CBHW070956120726
47910CB00004B/1262